Praise for *Gifts*

Wow! What an amazing collection of Christmas stories! I know not everyone likes short stories, but I love them, and this collection is amazing! Short stories are a different art form than novels. For a short story to be good, the writing needs to be tighter and crisper. And each of the 8 in this collection are very well written. One of the things I normally love about reading anthologies is discovering new authors. But that was not the case this time. I have read books by all of the contributors and had high expectations for this collection. I loved the anthology Secrets Visible & Invisible from the authors at Catholic Teen Books.

...For fans of the authors in this collection, you need to pick this book up to read their contribution. For readers who love remarkable stories, this collection is also for you. If you want some great reads that are clean Catholic\Christian fiction focused around the holidays, this is the book for you... (Full review on BookReviewsAndMore.ca)

Steven R. McEvoy, BookReviewsAndMore.ca

God bless these talented Catholic authors for putting together short stories, that are set in vastly different time periods, yet bring home the significance of humility, forgiveness, and the spirit of Christmas throughout the year. The thing that Catholics all over the world are taught to do is to live like Jesus, and lead with Love! If a smile or kind gesture will change a life, I know reading this book will change yours. Yes, Catholic families everywhere will need this in their collections!

Emily Davis, Catholic Blogger.

*No cartoon characters "saving Christmas" by making sure
presents happen, or mistletoe moments with less substance than
a snowflake here. These 8 stories entertain and edify the young-
adult reader and satisfy that Christmas craving for something
more, which can only be fulfilled by Jesus. Each story stands
alone, but many are connected to other work by the authors from
Catholic Teen Books.*

**Barb Szyszkiewicz,
Managing Editor, *Today's Catholic Teacher*
and Editor, CatholicMom.com**

~~~✝~~~
~~~

Gifts
Visible and Invisible

By Catholic Teen Books Authors:

Susan Peek
Katy Huth Jones
Carolyn Astfalk
Theresa Linden
Leslea Wahl
Cynthia T. Toney
T. M. Gaouette
Corinna Turner

First Edition

Cover design by T. M. Gaouette
Edited by Cynthia T. Toney

The following short stories are the work of the individual authors. Their inclusion here does not imply endorsement either by Catholic Teen Books or its individual authors.

Visit CatholicTeenBooks.com for more
title and author information.

Manufactured in the United States of America

Collection Copyright © 2019 Catholic Teen Books

Library of Congress Control Number: 2019913269

ISBN-13: 978-0997971859
ISBN-10: 0997971859

DEDICATION

For Saint Thérèse of Lisieux, model of love, who, in sharing her Christmas conversion story, wrote, "It was December 25, 1886, that I received the grace of leaving my childhood, in a word, the grace of my complete conversion . . . I felt charity enter into my soul, the need to forget myself and to please others; since then I've been happy!"

CONTENTS

1   THE OUTLAWS' FRIEND   1
- Susan Peek

2   IN THE STEPS OF A SAINT   25
- Katy Huth Jones

3   A PERFECT CHRISTMAS   53
- Carolyn Astfalk

4   OPERATION GIFT DROP   87
- Theresa Linden

5   CHRISTMAS ANGEL   121
- Leslea Wahl

6   SIGNS OF CHRISTMAS   143
- Cynthia T. Toney

7   JUST JESUS   165
- T. M. Gaouette

8   A VERY JURASSIC CHRISTMAS EVE   191
- Corinna Turner

FOREWORD

by Cathy Gilmore
Virtue Works Media

Do you read the "Foreword" in books? I don't often read them. Yet, I'm here writing one for you. So, I better make it good, right? Rather than preparing you for what is to come in this collection of short stories, I want to give you the reasons *why* you'll want to read them.

This is not your ordinary book, written by ordinary authors. This is a creative team of writers who could craft status-quo stories that conveniently leave out all reference to the ancient, yet timeless, Catholic faith in their work. But they don't. They could use cheap marketing tactics and saturate their writing with sexual explicitness and profanity. But they don't.

These authors don't *tell* you to "Dare to be different." They *show* you. They whisper to your soul in characters, dialogue, and settings that your life can be a GREAT story, one that includes a lifestyle of authentic Catholic faith. They take the time to craft scenes for you to imagine true goodness and redemption, in which the practical value of virtue is demonstrated on each page. And the bonus you receive is that in *GIFTS, Visible & Invisible*, you get all that wrapped up in a great Christmas vibe that you can climb back into anytime.

I invite you to get to know the authors of *Catholic Teen Books and enjoy their work.* Let them transform your assumptions and dispel the modern myths. Stories which affirm faith and virtue are NOT boring. Lives that are infused with the grace of faith and the valor of virtue are the greatest of adventures. I'm confident that you'll be surprised by how much you enjoy these stories which portray an array of genres, from warm family calamity to action-packed futuristic friendship.

Enjoy each story and its unique style, and ask yourself, how would you write that story? Could you tell that kind of story in your own way? We need courageous young Catholic writers. We need you to imagine and dream us a world where Jesus is welcome, the beauty of selfless sacrifice is valued, and the ugliness of evil can be overcome. What you imagine today can be tomorrow's reality. Read Catholic Teen books because we need you to write Catholic teen books... and change the world.

Cathy Gilmore
Founder / Executive Director, Virtue Works Media
Discover more great things to READ, WATCH & LISTEN
at VirtueWorksMedia.com

~~~†~~~
~~~

Every good gift and every perfect gift is from above,
coming down from the Father of lights with whom
there is no variation or shadow due to change.
(James 1:17)

THE OUTLAWS' FRIEND

by Susan Peek

Superior, Wisconsin
1896

"Barney, would you please listen to us?" his brother Gus begged. "This is crazy." He screwed up his face and slapped a hand to his forehead. "Just plain crazy!"

Barney opened his mouth to speak, but changed his mind.

Their other brother Pat set his jaw, crossed his arms, and blocked the front doorway. "At least don't leave till after Christmas." His eyes held a dare.

"He's right, Barn. What difference will three days make?" Gus joined Pat at the threshold, adding his own muscle and matching Pat's glare.

Their youngest brother Owen stubbornly hefted Barney's wooden traveling trunk—the one given him by, of all people, the outlaw Cole Younger of the notorious Jesse James Gang—and began to lug it back towards their bedroom.

Barney intercepted him, grabbing the handle with a huff. He instantly felt childish, as if they were kids fighting over a toy instead of the mature young men they were. "I can't believe this. My own brothers are ganging up on me."

For a few seconds, he and Owen grappled over the trunk.

"Look, we don't object to you going. But why leave Wisconsin tonight?" Owen clenched his teeth. Then his hand slipped, and he relinquished his grip with a sigh.

Barney nearly stumbled back with the sudden full weight of the trunk.

Owen extended his palms toward Barney. "Come on, Barn. Just stay one last Christmas. For Ma and Pa's sake." His eyes pleaded.

Barney glanced at Ma, pale-faced and silent across the fire-lit room, and a lump rose in his throat. For all he knew, he might never see her and Pa again, nor his nine brothers and four sisters. And that hurt. Ma stood at the table, busying her trembling hands by wrapping the bread, cheese, and salted pork that would serve as Barney's breakfast and lunch tomorrow. A delicate wood-carved nativity set, minus the much-awaited Infant, graced the corner behind her, next to a lopsided but charming Christmas tree. Hand-made decorations, holding years of precious memories, adorned its boughs.

"Ma . . . I . . . " Barney faltered, the words jamming in his throat. How could he leave them three days before Christmas?

The shutters rattled. Wind whistled through the cracks around the door as the storm outside grew in strength.

Ma raised her head and looked at Barney, her gentle eyes brimming with tears. For the first time since the Blessed Virgin had spoken to him thirteen days ago, Barney's resolve wavered. Could Ma see the anguish in his eyes? Did she understand that he must leave tonight, immediately, because if he didn't, he would chicken out and let the Blessed Mother down forever?

Not that Ma had any idea God's Mother was behind this.

Ma wiped her hands on her worn apron and shoved a loose strand of graying hair behind her ear. The corners of her mouth lifted slightly, as if she were attempting to smile, but a single tear escaped and slipped down her cheek. "A blizzard's blowing in. Please, Bernard, promise me you'll be careful." She always used his baptismal name. She swiped impatiently at the tear but didn't try to stop him from leaving. A woman who had borne sixteen children and buried two, Ma couldn't be selfish if she tried. But worry filled her eyes. Little wonder. Boarding a train with an oncoming blizzard wasn't normally a smart idea.

But nothing about this was normal.

To his shame, Barney couldn't hold her gaze. If he did, he would call this whole thing off. He let his eyes slide from Ma's distraught face and they snagged on Cole Younger's trunk. The irony of an infamous outlaw's trunk holding his possessions seemed suddenly comical and Barney had an irrational urge to laugh. God sure did have a sense of humor. Barney had carried the chest—a strange but sincere gift—out of the Minnesota State Prison a couple of years ago, never dreaming it would later be stuffed with his own belongings and hauled to a new prison four states away.

Because that's where Barney was headed. To prison.

For life.

With no parole.

His humor drained, replaced by a fresh stab of dread.

Near the door, Pat unfolded his arms in defeat and shook his head. "That train won't make it five miles from the station, let alone all the way to Michigan."

Gus added, "We're warning you, Barn, this is insane."

Seventy hours and hundreds of miles later, plowing through treacherous waist-high snow on a locomotive that a tortoise could outrace, Barney wondered if his brothers had, in fact, been right. This did seem insane. His heart sank with something akin to despair.

He leaned forward on the hard seat and strained, once again, to see out the ice-caked window. His exhausted reflection stared back at him with bloodshot eyes and three days' stubble. Beyond his mirrored face, snow slapped viciously against the glass pane. Beyond that, Barney could see nothing but deep darkness. This had to be the blizzard of the century. Howling wind rattled the carriage windows, while passengers huddled miserably under blankets and bulky coats. It was impossible to tell where they were. In the woods? Passing through a town?

Chugging through a bustling city?

Barney slumped back, his stomach knotting. How much longer? It was Christmas Eve. Would he make it to Detroit in time for Christmas Midnight Mass? Or even the morning Mass? At this rate, he would probably spend the most beautiful day of the year stuck in some impassible snowdrift on a cold locomotive. He should have listened to his brothers.

He sighed, wishing he could at least quiet his churning mind with sleep. He'd never been so tired in his life. He'd hardly slept since the train departed the station a lifetime ago. Surely they must be in Michigan by now, but with the train trudging so slowly, often only twelve miles an hour through the raging wind and snow, the journey was taking forever. What if they got stranded? What if the train derailed on the icy tracks? Which was worse—dying in a snowstorm on a frozen train or living the rest of his life in prison?

Stop calling it that, he ordered himself. *Sorry, Blessed Mother.*

Contrite, Barney fumbled in his pocket for his rosary beads. Sleep was impossible, so he might as well pray. His fingers groped around the worn material of his pocket, but the beads weren't there. Huh. Maybe they'd dropped to the floor.

Barney bent over and felt near his feet. His hand brushed the trunk under his seat. What would Cole Younger think if he knew where his trunk would wind up? Barney almost chuckled. In another cell, that's where.

Shoved under a narrow iron bed with a thin mattress and a single brown blanket. Not too dissimilar from Cole's own jail cell. There was a difference though. A big difference. Cole was locked up because he rejected God and broke His laws. Barney would relinquish his freedom because he wanted to save souls like Cole's.

The trunk held little. A couple of shirts, an extra pair of trousers. A razor. Why'd he bring the razor? Stubbornness maybe. The shirts and trousers would be useful for a few weeks before being replaced. The razor was useless already. Barney would never shave again.

He wouldn't even get to keep his name, let alone his smooth jawline.

Why are you sending me here, Blessed Mother? You know I have an aversion to beards!

It was a pathetic thing to be afraid of, growing a beard. But there it was, that darn-awful revulsion for the long, loathsome, bushy beards he knew his comrades would sport. And as if looking at them wasn't bad enough, he'd soon have one draped from his own face as well. Barney's tidy, clean-cut nature balked at the very thought.

He tried to picture Saint Francis with a flowing beard and recoiled at the image. *I blame you for this, Saint Francis. It's your fault, you know.* At that moment, his hand brushed something under his seat near the trunk. Must be his rosary. He swiped it up, sat back, and closed his eyes to pray.

The familiar motion of slipping the beads through his fingers calmed him, as it always did. He tried to

concentrate on the prayers, but his mind wandered from exhaustion, and instead of thinking of the mysteries of the rosary, his thoughts drifted back to his boyhood.

As often happened when he held his rosary, his memory locked on that one incredible, life-altering night many years ago. The remembrance of it was as vivid now as when it had happened. Barney had been especially tired that evening. After a long day of farm chores, he'd been tempted to dispense with his usual habit of praying the rosary before bed. He didn't give in. Swaying on his knees, fighting off sleep, he'd somehow managed to rattle off five decades before collapsing into bed. That night he had a dream.

He was hanging over a bottomless pit of fire, gripped with terror and about to fall in. Panic swelled. All was lost. Suddenly he glanced up and saw a giant rosary dangling overhead. He grabbed it in desperation and hung on for dear life.

He never fell into the pit.

After that night, the rosary became Barney's lifeline.

"Mister Casey? You awake?"

Someone was shaking Barney's shoulder. His eyes fluttered open. A man in a train uniform stood over him.

"This is your stop. Detroit, right? That's what your ticket says."

People moved in the aisle, stretching, yawning, hauling luggage from overhead bins. Icy air blasted through an open door a few feet away. Snow swirled into the carriage.

For a moment Barney fought to get his bearings. He must have nodded off while saying his rosary. How long had he dozed? Ten minutes, maybe? Nowhere near long enough to feel refreshed. If anything, he felt worse than before. Grogginess weighed him down. It was hard to sit up straight.

"Yes, yes. This is where I get off. Thank you." His mouth was dry, making the words come out too thick. His head pounded. All he wanted was to curl up in the seat, close his eyes, and sleep for a million years. "What time is it?" he asked.

The train attendant lifted a watch dangling from a chain near his front pocket. "Let's see. Santa will be squirming down the first chimneys in"—he squinted at the watch—"just over two hours, sir, give or take a bit."

Barney's heart sank. It was later than he thought. "Thank you."

The uniformed man nodded and moved on down the aisle, waking other dozing passengers.

Barney staggered to his feet. His legs wobbled, exhaustion overwhelming him. How far was Mt. Elliott Avenue from the station? Would he have to walk? Surely a big city like this would have streetcars running, even at night. Barney shrugged into his coat and stuffed his rosary into his pocket. His breath formed puffy clouds in the stale, freezing air. Leaning down, he hauled the outlaw's trunk from under his seat. Well, this was it. Prison time. No turning back now. Dismay swelled in his chest.

God, give me courage. He hefted the trunk into the aisle

and thought, *Offer this for Cole Younger. Someone needs to help save his soul.* Barney squared his shoulders. *Not just for Cole, Lord. For all those outlaws. They weren't such bad fellas. You know. They just need to find You.*

He drew a deep breath and gripped the trunk's handle with determination. Yes, he could do this for them.

Blessed Mother, here we go.

On the third ring of the bell, the door swung open. Just in the nick of time, otherwise Barney would probably have fallen asleep on his feet right there in the pile of snow. It was all he could do to keep his eyes open.

The first thing he noticed about the man on the other side of the door was his long, bushy beard. Barney involuntarily grimaced. The thing was downright atrocious. Who would do that to their face by choice?

Well, that fellow had no choice. And neither would Barney. Starting three days ago.

"Greetings in Christ, friend. How may I help you?" The man's eyebrow twitched up slightly, as if he was surprised by the appearance of a shivering, snow-dusted stranger on the doorstep at this incredible hour. Barney couldn't blame him.

"I'm sorry it's so late." Barney was too tired to think of anything better to say.

"Come inside. You must be freezing." The man's breath formed ice crystals on his beard when he spoke. He pulled the door wider, and Barney gratefully slipped in and stomped the snow from his shoes. His host rushed to relieve him of Cole's cumbersome trunk. "Are we expecting you?"

"Yes. My name's Bernard Casey. I've come from Wisconsin." Barney fumbled in his breast pocket for the letter tucked inside. "This is from Father Frey, the Provincial. I applied a few months ago." *Never expecting to actually be accepted!*

The friar took the letter and unfolded it. As his eyes skimmed its contents, his face lit up. He smiled, making the beard less unsightly. "Of course! Come in, come in!" He dragged over a scuffed wooden chair. "Sit down, please. You look ready to fall over. Let me fetch Father Casimir. He's the Guardian. He'll be so relieved you're here and safe."

"Thank you." Barney sat.

The friar spun to leave, his coarse brown robe swishing across the floor. After taking two steps, he paused and turned back around. "Have you eaten? I can cobble something up in the kitchen before we settle you in your cell."

"Thank you, Brother. That's very kind of you to offer. But I had something on the train."

The truth was, Barney was famished. Ma's packed lunch was a fading memory, and the meals on the train had been meager and unappetizing. But his desperation to sleep took precedence over his rumbling stomach.

Besides, he was too dismayed to eat. The thought of food made him almost ill.

Blessed Mother, why did you send me here? Sudden despair

and homesickness rushed full force upon him. *I don't want to be a Capuchin! Anything but a Capuchin!* He fought the ridiculous urge to bolt from the chair and run out the friary door.

Why, Mary, why?

After meeting Father Casimir and Father Gabriel, the Novice Master, Barney had been led to his cell at the head of the stairs. Getting settled could not have taken more than twenty minutes, but to Barney it felt like eternity. Drained of all strength, it took all his willpower to remain on his feet until the good Fathers were gone. When finally the door clicked shut behind them, Barney dropped onto the hard bed—coat, shoes and all—and laid his head against the lumpy pillow. The mere thought of undressing was beyond his strength. Finally, he could sleep!

He closed his leaden eyelids and took a few deep breaths, thinking sweet slumber would claim him instantly. But instead of relaxing, his muscles only tensed. His heart galloped in his chest; his stomach clenched as the reality crashed upon him. *I am truly here, entering an Order I don't really want to join!* Nothing against Saint Francis, of course, but who in their right mind would choose the Capuchins? Barney had just imprisoned himself for life, doomed to an itchy brown habit and slapped-together sandals, and nary a blessed razor again.

His lungs constricted, and something akin to panic poured over him. Why on earth had he applied to Saint Bonaventure's in the first place? Why had he not stayed in the seminary in Milwaukee? Sure, it had been hard, and the studies had worn him down. But *this?* Detroit? This whole thing was a mistake. A nightmare.

The desperately longed-for sleep that his body craved wouldn't come. Barney sat up, misery filling his heart. He knew it now—he definitely should've remained in the Milwaukee seminary. Heck, he should've stayed a lumberjack, like he'd been at fifteen, or a street-trolley driver a year later, or . . . or a Minnesota prison guard, for Pete's sake! He should've listened to Gus and Pat and Owen and never have boarded that wretched train in the first place. He belonged at home for Christmas, with Ma and Pa and his huge, loving, sprawling family.

The bleak thoughts crowded in and hopelessness clutched his heart with icy hands. Barney stood, agitated, his breath coming now in gasps. He had to leave. Had to get out of here. Cole's trunk sat near the bed, unopened, tempting. Everything was still packed. All he needed to do was—

Cole. Who would help save Cole's soul if Barney didn't try? Would anyone else here—*or anywhere?*—pray and sacrifice for the notorious outlaw, who, surprisingly, had a human and hurting heart hidden beneath all the dross and sin?

And what about the other jailbirds that Barney had come to consider his friends? A few of the more memorable ones flitted across his mind: Sam the Swindler, Little Joe, Rusty D. And of course Blackjack Charley. Who could forget Blackjack, with his cocky smile and lightning-fast draw—both with a card deck and, apparently, with a gun. Despite Barney's misery, a ghost of a smile twitched his mouth at the remembrance of his unusual friends. He'd been their prison guard, sure, but he'd shared their banter, their disappointments, even their baseball games. Their souls, wounded and disfigured by sin, were still unspeakably precious to God. Would those outlaws go to Hell because no one prayed for them? And that was only one prison in one tiny corner of the globe. What of the millions upon millions of sinners that needed converting? Hadn't Barney told Jesus countless times that he wanted to help save souls?

But . . . but he could save them from anywhere! Who said he had to grow a beard and shuffle around in floppy sandals in order to pray for souls?

God's Mother said. That's who!

Barney's insides tightened. Maybe he'd made the whole thing up. Had Mary actually spoken to him at Mass that day? He'd been sure at the time, but . . . he could have imagined it. Of course he could have! People imagined things all the time. After all, he was but a simple farm boy from the backwoods of Wisconsin. Why would Our Lady talk to him, of all people?

Barney paced the cell, wondering why he had written that letter to Father Frey all those months ago. His spiritual director had suggested he should, so Barney obeyed, never for a moment believing the Capuchin superior would reply, much less invite him to Detroit to join the Order. Now what? He'd gotten himself into a fine fix indeed.

Head hammering with doubts, Barney made his way to the curtainless window and stared into the dark yard outside. The blizzard had finally blown itself out, leaving the friary grounds draped in a thick blanket of virgin snow.

Go to Detroit.

Yes, Mary had said those words, and they could only have meant one thing: enter Saint Bonaventure's. Less than three weeks ago, on the Feast of the Immaculate Conception, Barney had heard those instructions as clearly as if the Queen of Heaven had knelt in the pew beside him and whispered in his ear. His novena was ending that very day. Together with Ma and his sister Ellie, Barney had spent nine days begging Mary to know God's will for his future. She had answered. She sent him to Detroit.

With a heavy heart, Barney returned to the bed. He had obeyed Heaven's command, but that didn't mean he was excited about it.

He kicked off his shoes, blessed himself with Holy Water, and crawled under the patched brown blanket, every bone in his body crying out for rest. He glanced one last time at the outlaw's trunk and an anguished groan escaped him.

This time when his head hit the pillow, he was out like a light.

At first, Barney wasn't sure what had awakened him. A jingling noise, like a little bell. Distant floating voices. Harmonious, like . . . singing. But not quite. He rubbed his eyes and sat up, trying to remember where he was.

The soft chanting drew closer; the voices swelled louder. He made out a few words.

Adeste fideles, laeti triumphantes . . .

Something was happening in the corridor.

Barney glanced at the clock on the small wooden table. Not quite midnight. He had slept barely an hour. Yet to his amazement, he felt fully refreshed and wide awake. The doom and despair that had gripped him earlier had completely vanished, replaced by tingling excitement. He swung out of bed and stuffed his feet into his shoes.

Venite adoremus, venite adoremus . . .

What was going on? Barney hurried to the door and cracked it open. His heart leapt at the sight.

A candlelit procession of smiling brown-robed friars flooded the hallway, their strong voices filling the air with joyful chant. Thick clouds of fragrant incense wafted from a golden censor swung back and forth by the thurifer in the lead. The Brothers grinned and nodded to one another, coming towards Barney's cell. Behind the thurifer, one of the friars carried a statue on a decorated pillow. Barney strained to see, then realized it was a slumbering Baby Jesus, on His way, no doubt, to be born in the church's crèche. A strange joy fluttered in Barney's chest.

The procession halted briefly at each door along the way, yet never breaking the rhythm of their swelling song. Each time, one of the friars would knock on the door and the cell's occupant would slip out, tacking himself to the tail of the line.

Barney's room was next. He couldn't help but grin. He gently closed his door, waiting for the ceremonious knock.

Tap, tap.

He reopened his door and waited as the friars filed past, flickering candlelight dancing on their faces and beards. For some reason the bushy beards didn't look so bad anymore. More than one Brother winked and nodded at Barney as they shuffled by. The heat from so many flames warmed him, both outside and in. Barney waited for the end of the line, then eagerly joined the procession.

He fell into step beside a young, bright-eyed friar with the first fuzz of a reluctant beard. Their gazes connected and they smiled at each other. Barney felt an instant bond with his new brother-in-arms.

He joined his voice with the others' song, following their soon-to-be-born King, and happiness flooded him. He wondered briefly what new name the Novice Master would give him when he took the habit in a few weeks' time. For Barney knew now, with certainty, that he would take the Capuchin habit. Some saint in Heaven, picked especially by God, was at this moment watching him, waiting with eagerness to become Barney's new patron. The thought of that saint, whoever he may be, sent peace and joy pulsing through Barney, unlike anything he had ever known.

Somewhere a bell tolled, ushering in midnight.

The Savior's birth had dawned.

Mary had been right, after all. Barney Casey belonged in Detroit.

It was Christmas, and Christ's Mother had brought him home.

Christmas Day, 1957

The old man trudged through the cemetery in the gently falling snow, clumsy in his new boots, as if his feet had forgotten how to behave in anything but government-issued shoes. He hugged his coat tighter around him against the chilly wind. It felt doggone strange to be wearing a nice, new woolen coat, actually chosen by himself and paid for with his own honest money at the department store last month in Minneapolis. Gee-willikers, how stores had changed in seventy years! Stepping through the door, Blackjack had felt like he'd been whooshed through a magic portal and dumped on another planet. All that fancy stuff hadn't even existed when he was sixteen years old! And it wasn't just the smart coat and toasty-warm boots, but *all* his new clothes. So many colors and styles not only boggled his mind but felt mighty unnatural on his old, frail body. He almost missed the ridiculous striped orange suit that had been his second skin since that fateful day in 1886 when he'd been young and stupid enough to draw his Colt .45 on a Minnesota lawman.

The world sure had changed since then. Automobiles and 'lectricity and running water right there in folks kitchens. Heck, they even had strange machines that sucked up dirt from the rugs these days. Who would've dreamed? Blackjack Charley shook his head.

But some things never changed. Like gratitude to a friend. Which was why he was making his clumsy way across a snowy Detroit cemetery in alien coat and boots. He had someone to say "Thank you" to. Not to mention "Merry Christmas."

The friars at the big building across the way had assured him it was an easy grave to find. There were always flowers there, they said, even in the dead of winter. Sounded like people came from all over America to honor his old friend's mortal remains.

Yep, the friars were right. That must be it, over there, near that large upright stone carving of Saint Francis of Assisi. Thanks to Barney, even *he* could recognize Saint Francis when he saw him! Usually the birds and wolf gave it away, but this carving was missing the animals. Instead it had a mountain with the setting sun, but the figure couldn't possibly be anyone but Saint Francis, wearing the rope and all. A few feet away from the towering saint, a bundle of frost-damaged poinsettias lay wilting and red against the glistening snow, next to a plastic bouquet of Christmas lilies. Had to be Barney's place. Someone had even placed a holiday wreath there, a circle of pine with what looked like little red berries and some kind of glittery gold ribbon woven around.

The old gunslinger shuffled through the flurrying snow and bent to his stiff knees by the grave. A pang of regret stabbed his gut. If only he'd been released half a year ago, he could have visited his former guard alive. He gently

brushed clumps of snow from the slab beneath him and read the words chiseled into the stone.

IHS
Rev. Francis Solanus Casey, O.F.M. Cap.
Born Nov. 25, 1870
Ordained July 24, 1904
Died July 31, 1957
Age 86 · Religious 60 Yrs.
R.I.P.

He blinked, surprised by the normalcy of the words. He didn't know what he'd expected, but it wasn't this. Barney wasn't even Barney anymore. He was Father Solanus. Of course Blackjack already knew that. All of America was talkin' about the Franciscan priest who'd spent the last sixty years as a humble friary doorkeeper, doing nothin' but answering the door and listening to folks' problems. But it wasn't just his kind words that had made thousands flock to Detroit to see him. It was the miracles. Stories had reached as far as the Minnesota State Penn. The sick had been cured, the blind given sight, the broken and crippled made whole—all by the prayers, or a simple touch, of the soft-spoken Capuchin buried beneath this frozen ground. Barney had worked so many miracles that the friars had eventually lost count, they'd told Blackjack with a chuckle.

Folks all over the country were already saying he'd be canonized one day. A fancy word—even fancier than the department store coat—and the ex-con knew little about such things. But what he did know was that his own life had been changed by having known the holy prison guard. He and Cole and all the rest of them—though the others were long dead—had, in some crazy way, been recipients of Barney Casey's power with the Almighty. Theirs were hidden miracles, of course. Things that would never be spoken about or printed up in one of those fancy pamphlets stacked on the desk inside the friars' building. But miracles nonetheless.

And somehow, Blackjack Charley felt certain that those were the best kind.

A lone tear slid down the outlaw's gaunt cheek.

With an unsteady hand, he dug in the bottomless coat pocket for his handkerchief. Imagine, a pocket this warm and deep! Would he ever get used to it? His gnarled fingers touched a tiny crucifix, a gift from his prison guard all those decades ago that he'd always kept. He even prayed with it every night, right before bed, he did. But right now, he needed the handkerchief. He pulled it out, wiped his eyes, and loudly blew his nose.

This would never do. Barney would never recognize him, sniffling and carryin' on like this. Where was his tough gun-toting self, the him that Barney had known, understood, and befriended?

He took a deep breath. Then he imagined looking his guard boldly in the eye, and he grinned with the cockiness with which he used to draw his six-shooter.

"Hey, it's Blackjack Charley. You remember me, don't you?" A lump lodged in his throat. He swallowed. Flakes of cold snow fell on his face. "I . . . I just came to say . . . well, on behalf of all the boys . . . Merry Christmas, Barney."

Something leapt inside the outlaw's heart, a little thump of joy, and he was sure that, from Heaven, his friend winked and smiled back.

₊₊*₊*

On November 18, 2017, Father Solanus Casey was beatified by the Roman Catholic Church and is now given the title Blessed. The cause for his canonization is ongoing. For more information about his holy life and miracles, including several full-length books about him, please visit www.solanuscenter.org.

ABOUT THE AUTHOR

SUSAN PEEK is a wife, mother, grandmother, Third Order Franciscan, and bestselling Catholic novelist. Her passion is writing stories of little-known saints and heroes. All her young adult novels have been awarded the coveted Catholic Writers' Guild Seal of Approval and are implemented into Catholic school curricula not only across the nation, but in Canada, Australia, and New Zealand as well. *Saint Magnus the Last Viking* and *The King's Prey: Saint Dymphna of Ireland* were both Amazon #1 Sellers among Catholic books. *The King's Prey* was also voted one of *Catholic Reads* TOP 10 BEST CATHOLIC BOOKS OF 2017 and was a Finalist for the 2018 Catholic Arts and Letters Award. *Crusader King* was featured as one of the 50 Most Popular Catholic Homeschooling Books in 2013. Susan lives in northeastern Kansas, where she can usually be found with her nose in a book, researching obscure saints to write about. Visit her at www.SusanPeekAuthor.com.

IN THE STEPS OF A SAINT

by Katy Huth Jones

Andrew shoved his hands into the pockets of his jacket and hunched down to make himself appear shorter. Just like at Holy Family Catholic Church, he towered over the other teens here at St. Francis of Assisi. Unlike his old youth group of seven friends, at least thirty kids packed the classroom, all talking excitedly with one another. He backed into the nearest corner, glancing toward the open door.

Could he leave without anyone noticing? It was only their first Sunday at St. Francis, after all. No one expected him to dive into youth group, right?

When he took a step toward the door, his younger sister, Mary, grabbed his arm.

"Oh, no you don't! Remember, Dad said it was best for us to just make ourselves at home." She beckoned a nearby girl. "Dora, this is my oldest brother, Andrew."

Dora gazed up at him with a giggle. "Hi, Andrew." She grinned, revealing braces, and then covered her mouth with her hands, giggling again.

Andrew grimaced, and Mary jabbed him with her elbow.

"Hi, Dora." He gave her a weak smile and eyed the door again.

A tall Hispanic man, maybe in his thirties, stepped inside wearing a big grin. Stacks of papers and booklets loaded his arms.

"Good afternoon! For those who are new, I'm about to put you on the spot. But first, my name is Wenche Gonzales, and I'm the leader of this youth group. Everyone, please take a seat. I have a special Christmas activity planned and need to pass out permission slips and song booklets." He handed a small stack to one of the girls and began passing out the larger sets of stapled papers.

A couple of the guys groaned while others pulled out folding chairs and set them up. Everyone except Andrew, Mary, and Dora continued their conversations.

Andrew excused himself from Dora and took one of the chairs at the back of the room. Mary said something to Dora before coming to sit beside him.

He watched the tall man move through the group. His unusual first name sounded like "Win-chee." Was that Native American? Andrew guessed it didn't matter, because he would call him Mr. Gonzales anyway.

When the leader reached Andrew and handed him a booklet marked *Christmas Carols*, Andrew looked up into the man's friendly dark eyes.

"You must be Andrew Novak." He shifted the booklets and shook Andrew's hand. "Welcome to St. Francis."

"Yes, sir. Thanks, Mr. Gonzales." Andrew maintained eye contact, wondering if this was how shorter kids felt looking up at him.

"You can call me Wenche." With a grin, he nodded at Andrew. "It'll be great to have someone with whom I can see eye-to-eye." He laughed and gave a booklet to Mary. "Mary Novak, right?"

Mary nodded. "That's right. How did you know?"

"I knew your family had just moved here from south Texas. Welcome to the Metroplex."

"I've heard people use that word." Andrew frowned. "Is it because Dallas and Fort Worth are so huge, and all the little towns have grown into bigger ones?"

"Yep, and now it's like one huge city instead of many smaller ones." Wenche finished passing out the booklets and maneuvered between the folding chairs back to the front of the room. "Ladies and gentlemen, let me have your ears, please."

After a few snickers everyone quieted down, and Andrew gave Wenche his full attention.

"First of all, we need to give Andrew and Mary Novak a warm St. Francis welcome." He pointed to them, and the room erupted in cheers and clapping.

Andrew's ears burned, and he ducked his head, but Mary waved with a smile. As soon as the others quieted, Wenche continued.

"Next Saturday morning at ten, we're going to go caroling at The Oaks Retirement Center. Two of our parishioners live there now, and they report that all the residents love young people and love to sing Christmas carols."

"But we're not a choir." One of the guys made a sweeping gesture to indicate everyone in the room.

"I can't sing." A girl near Andrew crossed her arms and stuck out her bottom lip.

Wenche held up his hands. "Doesn't matter. We're not performing; we're having a sing-along with the residents. Many of those people are lonely, especially during the holidays. Think of your grandparents: How would they feel if you weren't able to visit them during the Christmas season?"

"Mine are dead."

"Mine live next door."

Everyone started talking at once, but Wenche waved them to silence. "You're missing the point. I'm going to sing with the residents at The Oaks next Saturday, and I hope all of you will join me, 'cause I can't carry a tune in a bucket." A girl in front of Andrew raised her hand. "Yes, Annie?"

"Are we going to practice before we go?" Annie held up her booklet.

"I'm glad you asked." Wenche opened his book with a smile. "We're going to sing a few right now." Groans filled the room. "Turn to page eight, and let's start with 'Hark! The Herald Angels Sing.'"

Andrew turned to the designated page and slouched in his seat. Even worse than standing out because of his height, his voice hadn't finished changing, even after two years. If he sang too loudly, it still cracked. It was frustrating. He used to have a good voice and had sung in the choir at Holy Family.

Keeping his voice as soft as possible, he sang the familiar tune and prayed no one could actually hear him. After the first verse, Wenche waved them to stop.

"All right, that sounds great! Let's try one verse of a couple more. How about 'Silent Night' next? Page six."

After that, they sang the first verse of "Joy to the World," and everyone looked at Wenche expectantly.

"Can we sing them all?" Dora's voice sounded eager, but others moaned.

Wenche closed his booklet. "I think you're ready and able to give aid to the seniors at The Oaks."

"Hey, Wenche." One of the girls waved her hand. "There's a song in the back I've never heard of before, but it sure looks like your name. Good King Wensel-sauce?"

"Wenceslas. It's an easy song," Wenche promised. "And yes, Rosa, my parents named me Wenceslao, the Spanish version of that name, because I was born on his saint's day, which is September 28. Some of you forgot my birthday this year." A few of the others laughed.

Andrew flipped to the back of the booklet. He hadn't known this song was about a saint.

"How many of you have sung this carol?"

Only Andrew, Mary, and a couple others raised their hands.

"All right, let's sing it so everyone will be familiar with it on Saturday. It has a simple tune." He hummed a note.

but Annie raised her hand.

"Are we singing the whole thing, or just the first verse?"

Mary spoke up, which Andrew thought brave, even for her. "We should sing all of it, because it tells a story." She smiled at Wenche.

Wenche raised his eyebrows, obviously impressed. "Good idea, Mary. I'll start, and you jump in."

Although Andrew tried not to sing too loudly, he couldn't hide his voice among the others when so many struggled with the tune. Fortunately, his voice didn't crack this time. His sure pitch guided and seemed to encourage the other teens to sing along. Most of them stumbled over the unfamiliar words at first, but that made Andrew enunciate more clearly, like his old choir director had taught him. Mary was right; this song *did* tell a story.

By the time they reached the end, Andrew felt like he finally understood what this carol was all about. And King Wenceslas was a saint, a real person. Wenche's voice drew Andrew's attention back to him.

"Make sure your parents sign the permission form, and meet here next Saturday at ten sharp, so we can carpool and be ready to sing by ten-thirty." When the teens began to stand and fold their chairs, the youth minister added, "Don't forget to bring your song booklets and practice this week at home."

The noise of excited chatter crescendoed, filling the room. Andrew folded his chair and took both girls' chairs to put them all away.

"Must be nice to have such long arms." A shorter boy

nodded at him. "I'm Joe. Well, Joseph, but only my Mom calls me that."

"I'm Andrew. And sometimes it's handy to have long arms." Andrew shrugged and felt his face warm. "Sometimes they just get in the way."

The boys stacked the chairs and faced one another. Joe looked up with a lopsided grin. His eyes were such a pale blue, they looked almost like ice. But his tanned face was relaxed and friendly, so Andrew began to relax too.

"What grade are you in, Andrew?"

"Tenth. I'm going to Southwest High School tomorrow." First day in the new school, just in time for semester exams. Southwest was enormous compared to the school he'd attended back home. Home. This huge city was his home now, so different from the small town he'd come from.

"Me too!" Joe's grin widened. "Most of the kids here go to Our Lady of Sorrows, the nearest Catholic high school. I'm glad you're at my school." His gaze traveled to Andrew's arms, making him feel self-conscious. "Do you play basketball?"

"I tried, back home. But fortunately, the coach realized I wasn't cut out for it, even though I'm so tall. You know what he said? 'Wasted height.' I'm just glad no one else was standing nearby."

"Aw, man, that stinks." Joe jerked his head toward the door. "Come on, I'll introduce you to a couple of the guys I think you'll like a lot. They're not jocks, either."

Friday night, Andrew headed up to his bedroom immediately after dinner. He sat at his desk hunched over his Algebra II book, trying to solve a tricky polynomial.

"You look busy." Mary appeared in the doorway and leaned against the doorframe. "How was your first week of school?"

"Fine." He was glad he'd met Joe at youth group. They shared the same lunch period and English class. Seeing a few familiar faces had made starting a new school a bit easier.

"Are you ready for tomorrow?" Mary held up her song booklet.

"Oh." He'd forgotten all about it. With only a week's worth of classes before exams began, he'd had to study late into the evenings. He looked up at Mary's pleading eyes. "Maybe you'd better go without me."

Mary's eyes widened. "No way! You have the best voice of everyone. We need you! And, you're one of the few who knows how to sing 'Good King Wenceslas.'" She folded her arms and pretended to look stern. "You're coming with me."

Andrew couldn't help but admire his sister's determination. She was right; singing at The Oaks would be good for them both. With a sigh, he closed his Algebra book. "All right. I'll go tomorrow."

Mary grinned at him. "Thanks, big brother."

Andrew pulled out his photocopied song booklet and flipped through pages until he came to the last one. "Good King Wenceslas" was definitely different from the other songs.

Mary pointed to the first stanza. "I wonder why it says, 'the Feast of Stephen,' not Christmas?"

Andrew opened his laptop and searched *feast of Stephen*. "Hmm, it's the day after Christmas, the feast of the first Christian martyr, who was stoned to death. But how does he connect with Wenceslas?"

Mary leaned over and pointed to the bottom of the screen. "Look, there's Good King Wenceslas."

Andrew clicked on the picture and found an article describing the fascinating life of the saint. He lived in the early tenth century in a place called Bohemia, which sounded familiar to Andrew. He saw the word *Czech* and gasped.

"What?" Mary shifted her gaze to him. "What's wrong?"

He pointed to the paragraph in the article.

"Oh, he was Czech, like us. That's cool!" Mary grinned at him. "I'm glad you're going tomorrow. And not just because of your voice." She playfully punched his arm.

"My voice." Andrew sighed, remembering his old choir director. "Mr. Korenek said sometimes a boy soprano doesn't have a good voice after it changes."

"Pfft, what does Mr. Korenek know?" Mary rolled her eyes. "You still have a great voice. It will stop cracking. I know it will."

The corners of Andrew's mouth lifted despite himself. Mary sure could be fierce. "Thanks, Sis."

With a smile lighting her eyes, Mary shut Andrew's

door behind her.

Andrew looked back at his laptop. So, Good King Wenceslas was the patron saint of the Czech Republic. Why had his parents never mentioned that? Or had they, and he hadn't been paying attention?

Leaning back, Andrew thought about the small town in which he'd grown up. He knew his great-great-grandparents had emigrated from the Czech homeland to Texas, but that had happened so long ago, no one was still alive who remembered it. Old Mr. Blanik, their former neighbor, was the only person he knew who'd even been to the Czech Republic.

Many of Andrew's friends and classmates back home were also of Czech descent, but they never discussed it. Once a year the town held a Czech festival with dancing and polka music and sausage and homemade kolaches, but Andrew couldn't remember anyone ever mentioning Saint Wenceslas.

Before closing the laptop, Andrew decided to print out the article. The printer in the hallway began to churn.

When he took the internet article off the printer, he stared at the photo of a young man on horseback, a statue in the capital city of Prague. The Czech name for it was Praha, just like the even smaller town near his old home. Andrew wanted to learn more, but he had to finish Algebra. He put the papers on his desk, resolved to get back to Wenceslas as soon as he could.

The next morning, Dad stayed with the younger

children while Mom drove Andrew and Mary to St. Francis. Andrew let Mary sit in front, and she and Mom chatted while he watched out the window.

At a stoplight, Andrew saw a sad-looking man wearing worn clothing and a thin jacket sitting on a piece of cardboard in the middle of the sidewalk. His dark hair and beard were unkempt, and he wore no hat, though a brisk cold wind scattered trash from a nearby alley. Andrew had never seen anyone who looked so hopeless.

"Mom." He leaned forward. "Is that a homeless person?"

She glanced back at Andrew from the driver's seat. "Yes, it is. Your father says there are many of them here because several major highways intersect in the Metroplex, bringing transients from all over the country."

"Transients?" Mary twisted in her seat in front of Andrew so she could be part of the conversation.

"People with no permanent home who are always traveling from place to place." The light turned green, so Mom had to face forward again.

"How do they live?" Andrew watched the homeless man until he was out of sight. "Can't they find a job?" When Dad lost his job after the factory shut down, it only took him a month to find another one.

"Oh, honey." Mom's voice sounded sad, and Andrew jerked his head toward her. "Most of them can't hold a job."

"Why not?" That man had looked young and strong enough to work.

"Many have an addiction to drugs or alcohol."

Andrew's gut twisted in sympathy. He remembered Bobby Volnak, who'd gone to a graduation party last spring and gotten wasted. While driving home under the influence, Bobby had lost control of his car, killing himself and the elderly couple he'd hit head-on. Was that how some of those homeless people had gotten trapped by drugs and alcohol? When they were young and tried it at a party? The word wasted had a whole new meaning now.

"Mom, why doesn't someone help these people? Where are their families?" Andrew shifted in his seat.

"Unfortunately, not everyone has family or friends they can turn to. And if they're addicts, they have to ask for help. No one can force them into rehab."

The discussion ended as they pulled into the parking lot of St. Francis. Four other cars waited near the door of the Parish Life Center. Wenche stood chatting with some of the parents, while a group of kids hung out nearby, Joe among them.

When Andrew climbed out of the back seat, Joe waved and sauntered toward him.

"Hey, Andrew!" Joe smiled at Mary as she hurried past to greet Dora. "I need to stand next to you at the senior center, since you actually know how to sing."

Andrew shrugged. "I used to sing pretty good."

"What do you mean, 'used to'? You have the best voice I've ever heard, well, for a kid, I mean. You should sing louder."

Mary and Dora approached them. "That's what I keep

telling him too." She stuck out her tongue. "See, I'm not the only one."

Andrew shook his head, and his face warmed. He opened his mouth to reply, but Wenche called them to attention.

"I thought there'd be more of you coming, but we'll do our best." Wenche gestured to the waiting parents. "We can recruit our drivers too." He grinned at them and held up his song booklet. "Ladies and gentlemen, start your engines, and let's get this show on the road."

Andrew squeezed into the back seat of a smaller car to sit beside Joe and another boy. As soon as he did, he wished he'd found a larger vehicle. His knees bent painfully against the back of the front seat.

"How far is this senior center?" He tried not to sound whiny, but he couldn't remember being this uncomfortable in a long time.

"Not far." Their driver, who was someone's mother, started the car and backed out of the parking space.

"Shouldn't we wait for Wenche?" The girl in the front seat sounded anxious.

"I know the way." The driver waved at the others. "Somebody's got to get there first, right?"

Unlike his Mom, this woman was a more aggressive driver. When she sped around a corner, the force pushed Andrew into Joe, making his stomach lurch. He couldn't tell for sure if the car had taken the turn on two wheels.

Thankfully, there were just a few more blocks, and their driver parked in front of The Oaks Retirement Center. The three-story building didn't look like a nursing home; more like a fancy hotel. Andrew unfolded himself from the back seat and stood with the others on the front porch. A gust of wind made Andrew shiver. He thought of the poor homeless man sitting outside in the cold. Did he sleep on that cardboard?

Finally, the rest of their group arrived. Warm air with the odor of disinfectant greeted them as they stepped into The Oaks. They followed Wenche to the lobby and waited while he spoke to the woman at the front desk. Andrew looked up at the ornate chandelier. Sunlight entered through a tall window, refracting in the crystals and creating rainbows on the walls.

Wenche then led them down a short hall to a large dining room. A few of the elderly residents already sat in chairs or wheelchairs, and more were slowly walking in or were being pushed in wheelchairs by the staff.

Andrew had the same queasy feeling he used to get whenever he sang a solo back home. If he didn't calm down, his voice would crack for sure. He reminded himself this wasn't a performance.

Once everyone was in place, Wenche thanked them for coming and invited them to sing along. Then he turned and said quietly, "We'll sing every song in our booklet, front to back."

They began with "O Come All Ye Faithful," which everyone knew, and the residents sang out with more enthusiasm than Andrew expected. He smiled at one lady in the front, who closed her eyes and sang off-key with joy on her glowing face.

Singing with these eager seniors was much more satisfying than Andrew could have imagined. They knew the words to all the carols by heart. All except the last one, which was "Good King Wenceslas." Only a few of the residents were confident enough to sing out, so Andrew's voice was heard above all the rest. This time, however, he made a conscious effort to forget about himself and think only about the carol's story of the saint's kindness to a poor man "gath'ring winter fuel."

At the end of the song, the residents clapped, and Joe grinned up at Andrew.

"Thanks for singing out." Joe pointed to his songbook. "You made me sound good."

Wenche encouraged all of them to meet the residents and visit with them for a little while before heading back to the parking lot.

"Who's ready for pizza?" Wenche rubbed his hands together. Everyone answered at once.

"Pizza?"

"I'm always ready for pizza."

"Where are we going?"

Wenche opened his car, and three boys piled inside. "Mrs. Novak should have pizza waiting for us at the church."

Andrew met Mary's gaze, but she shrugged. So that's why Mom didn't come with them. Reluctantly, Andrew returned to the same small car and twisted himself into the back seat.

On the way back, the others chatted while Andrew watched out the window. When they turned onto a major street, he noticed two more homeless men sitting huddled together, sharing a blanket. Suddenly, the words of the last carol leaped into Andrew's mind: "when a poor man came in sight, gath'ring winter fuel."

When Saint Wenceslas saw a poor man in need, he did something about it, even though it was bitterly cold. Back home, there were no homeless people, but neighbors helped neighbors whenever anyone had a need. What could Andrew do for the poor people in his new city? What did they need most?

He couldn't stop thinking about it the whole time their group sat around folding tables, stuffing themselves with pizza. Andrew studied the slice in his hand. Had he taken daily food for granted his entire life? What about warm clothing, a jacket, socks, shoes? He'd never lacked for anything. Then one of the boys spoke loudly, interrupting his thoughts.

"Hey, I heard a joke about Good King Wenceslas."

"What is it?" Joe leaned on the table.

"What kind of pizza does Wenceslas like best?" The other boy smirked.

Joe thought a minute and shrugged. "I don't know. Do you know, Andrew?"

Andrew shook his head, so the boy answered.

"Deep pan, crisp and even. Get it?" He broke into song, dreadfully off key. "When the snow lay round about, deep and crisp and even."

Everyone groaned. Andrew was too distracted to react. He got up and went to talk to Wenche.

"Hey, Andrew, what's up?" Wenche gestured to the empty seat across from him, and Andrew sat down.

"I've been noticing lots of homeless people since we moved here." He clasped his hands together beneath the table. "I never saw one before. Back home, everyone had family or neighbors to help out."

Wenche took a sip of his soda. "There are a lot of homeless in the Metroplex, especially near the bigger downtown areas."

"I wondered if there's something we could do for them. I mean, even Wenceslas gave the poor man food and wine and firewood." Andrew leaned his arms on the table. "I know blankets would be too expensive, but what about socks? And something easy to eat? Maybe even a bottle of water?"

Wenche's eyes sparkled, and he grinned. "Andrew, that is a great idea. I've only helped raise money for the homeless shelters, never thinking there might be something else I could do personally. But now that I think about it, I've heard of others making 'blessing bags' to pass out to the homeless. Did you want to do this as a project of the youth group?"

Andrew's eyes widened. "I'm just the new guy."

"So, you changed parishes." Wenche cocked an eyebrow. "What difference does that make?"

"I don't want to put anyone out." Andrew hunched down, then straightened again and met Wenche's gaze

This was important enough to put aside his timidity. "If a bunch of us got together, we could help more than one person, which is probably all I could help if I did it myself."

Wenche pulled out his cell phone and searched for a few minutes. Then he turned the screen so Andrew could read about different ideas for items to put inside a gallon-sized plastic bag.

"Hey, everyone, gather around. Andrew has an idea for us." Wenche motioned with his hand.

While the others flocked to the table, Mary, Dora, and Joe leaned over Andrew's shoulder to see what he was looking at.

"Blessing bags?" Joe sounded puzzled, and Andrew raised his head to answer. Wenche beat him to it.

"Help for the homeless." Wenche nodded at Andrew, encouraging him to speak.

"We could pick five or six useful things to put inside a large plastic bag and divide them up among all of us so it wouldn't cost too much. Then we could get together, fill the bags, and deliver them." Andrew pictured the sad young man he'd seen earlier and wondered if he would still be in the same general location.

"How many bags were you thinking to fill?" Wenche studied the image on the phone's screen.

"As many as we could. After all, socks and peanut butter crackers and granola bars come in packages with at least six, I think." Andrew frowned. Wouldn't that make each item less costly? "Surely we could afford to make

enough bags for the homeless people nearest to us?"

"When I drive downtown, sometimes I see a couple dozen, at least." Wenche bit his lip, thinking. "We have a large enough group that we could ask each family to bring three boxes of six items, whether food or toiletries or bottles of water."

"What if everyone buys granola bars?" Mary scuffed her feet. "Could we make a list of specific things and have everyone sign up?"

"Sounds great, Mary." Wenche pointed to a nearby shelf with office supplies. "Bring me a piece of paper and a pencil, please." After he took them from her, he wrote "Blessing Bags" at the top and drew a perpendicular line down the middle of the page.

"Okay, Andrew, we have socks, bottles of water, peanut butter crackers, granola bars." Wenche finished writing. "What else do we want in our blessing bags?"

Andrew glanced at Mary, who nodded encouragement. "I know gloves are too expensive, but what about those little bottles of hand cleaner?"

"Or those individually-wrapped hand wipes." Dora's face shone with enthusiasm. "We got a box of them, and there were tons inside."

"My grandma crochets hats." Joe pulled one from his coat pocket and put it on. "If we give her some yarn, she can make one of these in less than an hour."

"Does she have any friends who crochet?" Mary held out her hand for the hat, and Joe let her see it.

"My grandmother knows how." Rosa pantomimed

using a crochet hook. "She tried to teach me, but I'm not good enough. I think Tia Juanita can, though."

Everyone started talking at once until Wenche held up his hands. "Why don't we put out the call at church tomorrow, gather the items the following Sunday, and meet that afternoon to put the bags together?"

Andrew grinned, warmed to his heart that the others were so interested in helping. "And then we can deliver them? By Christmas?"

"Sure." Wenche clapped a hand on Andrew's shoulder. "And if not by Christmas Day, definitely by the day after. You know, the Feast of Stephen." With a wink, he turned to help clean off the tables.

On the way home, Mary shared her excitement over Andrew's idea, making sure to give him the credit, even though that part didn't matter to him.

Mom glanced over her shoulder. "That's a wonderful idea, Andrew, but don't expect a lot of participation from the others. Most families don't have a lot of extra money, especially this time of year."

"I'm not, Mom." He put his hand on Mary's seat and leaned forward. "In fact, I was wondering if, instead of buying me a Christmas present this year, you help me buy a few things so I can at least make up five or six of those bags for homeless people."

At the red light, Mom looked back at him, her eyes shimmering. "You're committed to this, aren't you?"

Andrew thought about the poor man in the Wenceslas

carol. "Yes, I am."

The following Sunday, Andrew waited anxiously to see what the others would bring for the blessing bags. He'd already determined to find a way to fill more bags on his own if turnout was meager.

Wenche opened the door to the room where the youth group met, but pulled it shut behind him before Andrew could go in. He frowned. Was it that bad?

"Prepare yourself, Andrew." Wenche looked solemn, making Andrew's heart sink.

"Okay." He swallowed his disappointment. After all, people had to think about their own families at Christmas.

Slowly, Wenche opened the door. Andrew was afraid to look inside.

When he did, his mouth fell open. Two long tables were piled with packages of socks, cases of bottled water, boxes of granola and protein bars, small cans of fruit and meats, bottles of hand sanitizer, even some gloves. And a colorful stack of knitted hats lay at one end.

"Wow!" Tears pricked Andrew's eyes. He never dreamed the people at St. Francis would be so generous.

Wenche was grinning so widely, Andrew thought his face would split open. "Your idea lit a fire in this parish, Andrew."

"We can put together enough blessing bags to give to all the homeless in Tarrant County." Andrew couldn't wait to get started.

"Not all the homeless." Wenche's voice was gentle.

"But certainly quite a few of them."

"Let's organize all this stuff so we can put the bags together this afternoon." Andrew picked up all the boxes of gallon-sized plastic bags and moved them to the end of the table. Then he tore open the nearest box of protein bars.

In twos and threes, the other teens entered the room with exclamations of surprise and got to work. Before Andrew knew it, they'd assembled close to a hundred blessing bags. Wenche found a few empty boxes to hold them.

"Can we deliver some now?" As satisfying as it was to put the bags together, Andrew knew they weren't of use to anyone until they were placed into the hands of the homeless.

"We can do this more than one way." Wenche addressed the group. "Either we divide up the bags and you deliver them with your families whenever you see a needy person around the city, or we can meet again on Saturday and deliver them in teams."

As much as Andrew would love to team up and deliver them all at once, he saw the benefit of each family having several bags on hand to pass out whenever they saw a need.

"It makes more sense for us to divide up the bags, don't you think?" Andrew scanned the faces of all his new friends. "We all see homeless in different locations, so that way we can reach as many as possible."

Everyone agreed. Wenche made sure each family got a

box of blessing bags. The leftover items remaining on the table would be a good start toward filling other bags in the future.

"Where can we store this?" Andrew looked hopefully at a small cabinet in one corner of the room.

"It might be safer if one of us took it all home." Wenche raised his brows. "You know how crazy a hungry teen boy can get."

Andrew's Mom stood in the doorway. "You want to hold onto this, don't you, Andrew?"

"Could we?" Andrew nodded at the table. "I mean, I do eat a lot, but I'm not crazy." He looked back at Mom. "Anyway, if you buy me the rest of the supplies as my Christmas present, I can fill even more bags."

Wenche crossed his arms and smiled. "Don't tell anyone I said this, but you are rather amazing, Andrew Novak."

Andrew shook his head. "It wasn't me. I was just following in his steps."

"Huh?" Wenche looked puzzled.

"Wenceslas. I got this idea from him." He gave Wenche a lopsided smile.

Nodding, the youth leader squeezed Andrew's shoulder. "And just like the footprints of Saint Wenceslas warmed his servant as he trod in the snow, you've encouraged us all to 'tread more boldly' to help those in need."

On the way home, Andrew noticed the same sad young

man sitting on the cardboard. "There's the homeless man I saw before. Please stop, Mom, so I can give him one of the bags."

Mom found a safe place to pull over, and Andrew picked up a blessing bag. He made sure it contained a hat and a pair of gloves. Then he slowly approached the young man so as not to startle him.

It wasn't until Andrew stood right next to him that the homeless man looked up. Andrew squatted down to be closer to his eye level. He held out the bag.

"My name is Andrew. I hope you'll find these things helpful." He stared into the man's sad eyes and gave him a smile.

For a moment, Andrew thought he would refuse the bag. But he slowly reached out a trembling hand and accepted the gift.

"I notice you don't have a hat. There's a warm hat inside that a kind lady made for you." Andrew slowly stood and backed away. "Merry Christmas."

The man opened the bag and took out the hat. After running his hand over it, he pulled it on his head and gave Andrew a thumbs up. Andrew waved and got back in the car.

"Thanks, Mom." He watched the homeless man until they turned the corner, then leaned back and closed his eyes. Now he knew for sure what the final line of the Wenceslas carol meant:

"Ye who now will bless the poor shall yourselves find blessing."

₌₌*₌*

If you're interested in learning more about "Good King" Wenceslas, whose care for the poor inspired John Mason Neale to write the Christmas carol about him, there's a fictionalized account of his inspiring life. The historical novel *Treachery and Truth: A Story of Sinners, Servants, and Saints*, published by Pauline Books & Media, tells the story of Saint Wenceslas from the point of view of his servant, Poidevin. The incident mentioned in the Christmas carol can be found there, though there is so much more to discover about the kindness and courage of this young ruler, whose faith shone as a beacon of light in the Dark Ages.

ABOUT THE AUTHOR

KATY HUTH JONES has been obsessed with Wenceslas and all things Czech since a friend first gave her a short book about his life more than thirty years ago. Since then, she and her husband have visited the Czech Republic twice, literally walking in the steps of the saint, and now she is trying to learn the difficult Czech language. Thankfully she has found a few Texans who speak it, since many descendants of Czech immigrants still live in Texas.

Jones has been a published children's author since 1992, but now her favorite job title is "Grandma."

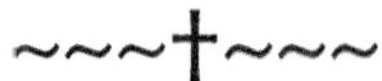

A PERFECT CHRISTMAS

by Carolyn Astfalk

Hands pressed to my ears, I tried to block the cacophony of Christmas chaos from the living room. "I'm trying to balance this equation!" I yelled, doubtful anyone heard me.

From my vantage in the dining room-cum-homeschool classroom, I twisted strands of my tawny brown hair around a finger and narrowed my eyes at my little sister, three-year-old Lily, as she pounded the ivory piano keys with chubby hands. Probably sticky with traces of Nutella and peanut butter.

I tightened my fist on a perfectly sharpened #2 pencil, tempted to snap it in two. "Stay off my *piano*," I shouted.

Five-year-old Peter scream-sang "Jolly Old Saint Nicholas" out of sync with Lily's pounding while twirling himself in several yards of shiny gold garland. Wearing discount store fingerless gloves—like he always did—he wiggled his bare fingers, arms outstretched. With his head tilted back, he sang in Yuletide oblivion induced by the contents of the now-empty candy package under the table no doubt. Those chocolate-covered cherries had more sugar than any item in the pantry. I'd bet on it.

Mom squeezed by my chair with the toddler, Clementine, propped on her hip and tugging at her shoulder-length brown hair.

Poor Clementine. The sweet little thing had spent the night barking like a seal with her second case of croup in two months. I knew because despite being fifteen, I bunked with Lily, and our room shared a wall with Mom and Dad's bedroom, where Clementine and the new baby, Linus, slept.

I'd begged my parents not to name the poor kid Linus, but did they listen? Now my precious baby brother would spend a lifetime listening to lame attempts at jokes like "hey, where's your blanket?" or "what's your nickname—Sweet Babboo?"

My only consolation lay in the fact that if my parents were determined to name their progeny after the roster of popes, they'd at least had the sense to bypass Cletus. How Lily and I escaped the fate of our siblings, I did not know.

"*Your* piano, Marigold?" Mom tossed one of Dad's dress shirts onto the mending pile at the end of the couch.

While not emblazoned on any lists pertaining to the papacy, my name still, in my opinion, rots.

I scowled at Mom's back. Did she know it was covered in spit up?

She trudged forward, penetrating the maelstrom in the living room, and unraveled Peter from the twisted garland.

"It's the family's piano, not yours," Mom said, her tone, like everything else about her these days, exhausted.

"But I'm the only one who actually knows how to *play* it." I protested, desperate to have *something* in this overtaxed, over-populated household that I could claim as my own.

Mom slipped behind me again. A crash-bang of chords sounded as Lily dismounted from the piano bench. She joined Peter in trying to destroy our new Christmas decorations. The ones we'd bought on sale that morning to festoon our drab artificial tree, tomorrow being Christmas Eve and all.

I closed my textbook and lay the pencil on top of it. With little chance of completing a coherent thought, how would I ever master redox reactions?

Mom returned, apparently unable to ignore Lily and Peter's antics.

While she dealt with the little ones, which seemed to take 98 percent of her time lately, I shuffled to the picture window overlooking the backyard. Brown grass dotted with patches of mud sat dully beneath a pumice-gray sky in the shadow of the woods at the rear of my parents' property.

In fifteen Christmases, I couldn't remember a single white one. *C'mon God, give us a dusting, at least.* I wasn't asking for a miracle, just a nudge. This was Pennsylvania, not Hawaii, after all. We *did* get snow.

Pressing a twisted lock of hair between my lips, I anticipated Christmas with delight—snow or not—dorky as that may sound. Somewhere around my tenth birthday, Christmas eclipsed Halloween as my favorite holiday. I'm sure it had nothing to do with the neighbor boy, Benny Esposito, jumping out from behind their row of half-dead arborvitae trees wielding an axe. A plastic axe, granted, but it frightened me so badly I screamed like the little girl I was. My breaths coming in short, shallow bursts, I bolted, my pink tight-clad legs pumping hard and my sparkly white tutu catching on prickly bushes as I barreled down the path to home.

More than anything, I wanted this Christmas to be *perfect*. Hence my dissatisfaction with little siblings destroying items intended for decoration. Every day, reasons mounted for this not being the ideal holiday. Dad was stuck out of town in Colorado, where it *was* snowing. Linus was colicky, Clementine was croupy, Lily was . . . Lily, and Peter was crazy—not in a mental illness kind of way, but more like a loopy weirdo way.

Poor Mom had to deal with all of them. And me, though I tried not to be *too* demanding. To help her out, I'd taken the liberty of creating a master agenda for Christmas baking, an itemized list for Christmas shopping, and a whiteboard filled with fun ideas from Christmas caroling to a neighborhood light-peeping expedition.

My gaze snapped to the stairs. Linus cried high-pitched and frantic from above, the insistent demand of an infant awakened by all the noise and realizing he was both alone and hungry.

"I'll get Linus," I called to Mom.

Flopped on the couch with Clementine climbing all over her, her call of "Thanks, hon," exuded gratitude.

Things would settle down tomorrow. The little ones would sleep better tonight, and Lily and Peter couldn't maintain their frenzied pace much longer.

I imagined Christmas morning—the sweet aroma of sticky buns in the oven and the crinkling of festive wrap being ripped from presents—as I jogged up the hardwood stairs, dodging a haphazard assemblage of rubber dinosaurs arranged around a miniature tea set.

Inside Mom and Dad's dimly lit bedroom, I found Linus safely half-swaddled in his co-sleeper, his scrunched-up face red with frustration. "I got you, buddy." I scooped him up and arranged him carefully against my shoulder, murmuring softly and patting his bottom.

A rush of pure joy shuddered through me. Yes, my little brothers and sisters aggravated me, but they also wowed me. Their perfect little bowed lips, wispy lashes, and silly laughter. I couldn't help but love them. I only wished they'd get with the program once in a while and cooperate. Cherubs had their proper place in a perfect Christmas too—a silent spot in the manger tableau, mind you, but a spot nonetheless.

As I stepped into the hall, my gaze snagged on the open closet where my Christmas dress hung. Money was tight this year, as always, but my aunt had delivered a bag of hand-me-downs where I'd found the perfect dress for my first time at Midnight Mass. The zipper in the back needed to be replaced, but Mom was a whiz with the sewing machine and had agreed to repair the garment.

The A-line dress made of crushed black velvet featured sparkly, silver-threaded trim. I'd wear my hair up in a bun and borrow Mom's silver dew drop earrings. Maybe we'd take pictures after Midnight Mass like we usually did Christmas morning, with a wall of red poinsettias and the altar behind us.

Linus rubbed his face against my chest as I carried him downstairs.

The bags under Mom's eyes disappeared as she smiled and extended her arms to accept the warm bundle from me. "Hey, sweet baby," she cooed. "Did you sleep well?"

"So, Mom," I said, plopping beside her onto an assortment of ripped, button-less garments—the mending pile. "Can you get that zipper on my dress fixed by tomorrow? 'Cause carols start a half hour before Midnight Mass, and we should leave early so we get good seats."

Her deep sigh as she fussed with her shirt and allowed Linus to nurse signaled regret.

Dread tightened my stomach.

"Honey, I'm sorry, but—"

"No, Mom." I waved my open hands in a frantic gesture, tension tightening my neck and shoulders. "You said we could go, I—"

"Linus has got his days and nights mixed up, Clementine still isn't well, and I don't know *what* time your dad is going to be home." She offered me a pitying smile then turned back to the baby happily suckling.

I bit the inside of my cheek to keep from exploding.

Couldn't I do *one* grown-up thing? No, not even grownup—age-appropriate. And it wasn't like I wanted to do something reckless or stupid. It was Mass, for goodness sake. A church service!

I love my family, I do. But I'm fifteen, and I'm tired of every sentence I utter being interrupted. I'm tired of being awakened in the middle of the night because my roommate wet the bed. And for the love of all that is good and holy, I'm tired of the house smelling like dirty diapers!

"But, Mo-o-om," I whined. Ironic, because whining sat at the top of the list of annoying things the little ones did.

Linus batted at Mom's face, the corner of his lips turning up as he nursed, while Mom gazed at him with a look of pure love. On the other side of the room, Clementine knelt watching Peter and Lily build an elaborate fort with wooden blocks.

Intellectually, I understood Mom's reluctance. Emotionally, well, I couldn't accept it, stubborn soul that I was.

"If Dad's not back, I'll help you." I glanced at the kids. "They're just gonna sleep in the pew, anyway."

"The answer is no, and I'm done discussing it." Mom patted my knee, which I'm sure she meant to be loving but that felt condescending nonetheless. "I'd like to go at midnight, too, and for you to experience it, but it's just too much this year. Next year—"

I sprung from the couch, which was no small feat considering the saggy cushions that should've been reupholstered ten years ago. And mom's weight sucking me down. Not that I would go *there*, even if I was angry with her.

"Next year? By then you'll probably have adopted six kids from Zimbabwe and taken in five stray cats. I'll *never* get to go!" I had nothing to do upstairs, but that kind of statement required a dramatic exit, so without waiting for Mom's reaction, I stomped from the room and raced up the steps, purposely crashing the dinosaur tea party in the process.

I tried slamming the bedroom door, but Lily's terry cloth cover-up hanging from the doorknob prevented the door from closing. After three firm shoves, it closed with a soft click.

Huffing in anger, I flopped onto my bed and buried my head under a pillow. Christmas was ruined, and I couldn't pretend anymore that it wasn't.

Mom hadn't bought a single item on my cookie ingredient list. The fake, bagged tree still lay outside the attic door where Dad had left it before going out of town. And who knew if my parents had done any shopping? Although I'd asked them at least a dozen times to take me to a discount store to do my own shopping, somehow — surprise, surprise — they hadn't found the time.

And it wasn't just that I was all caught up in the commercial side of Christmas. Like the littlest Who in Whoville, I knew Christmas was about more. I'd done Advent, helping the little kids with the Jesse tree, lighting our wreath, and reading the kids Bible stories. Heck, I'd even used the little pamphlet Mom had given me, one from the back of church that recommended readings and reflections and things like fasting and meditating on death. Yes, death, 'cause of the second coming of Jesus and all. My Advent preparation had been thorough, bordering on Lenten asceticism, if you asked me, and darned if I wasn't going to be at that Midnight Mass, belting out the "Gloria" we hadn't sung since around Thanksgiving.

Beneath the pillow, I groaned and pushed back the hot tears stinging my eyes. When I cried, my eyes grew tired and my contact lenses felt weird. What good would tears do anyway? With the amount of crying that happened in this house on a daily basis, displays of blubbering did not sway Mom.

I must've dozed off—that's what late-night self-promises of "just one more page" got me—because the next thing I knew, the trill of a cell phone sounded through the bedroom wall. Mom must've left her phone up here when she put Linus down for his nap.

Tossing the pillow at the head of my bed, I rushed into my parents' bedroom and grabbed the phone from the nightstand. Dad's name showed on the display, so I swiped my finger across the screen and answered it.

"Hey, Dad." I forced a little lilt into my voice, not wanting to sound sullen and be subjected to a series of questions about what was wrong. Things always hit the fan, so-to-speak, when Dad traveled. Overflowing toilet, raccoon in the garage loft, dead car battery, you name it. My disappointment didn't even register on the work travel-home emergency chart.

"Marigold? Wassup, sweetie?" Dad seemed to be half-shouting over background noise. The blare of multiple televisions faded behind hoots, hollers, and clapping.

"Not much. Where are you?" I'd hoped he was on his way home by now.

"I'm, uh, at the airport." Muffled noises then raucous background laughter. "I should be boarding the plane in an hour or so."

I pulled the phone from my ear and glanced at the time. I *had* fallen asleep. Dinner would be in about twenty minutes. By the time Dad got home, it would be late. Maybe midnight.

"Can I talk to Mom?" Something about Dad's voice sounded funny. Off. But I couldn't pinpoint what.

"Yeah, sure," I said, galloping down the steps.

I found Mom in the kitchen, Linus strapped to her back, stirring a pot of pasta in boiling water.

"It's Dad," I said, handing her the phone and taking the wooden spoon from her.

"Oh," she said, wiping a hand on her pants. She stepped away from the stove but not out of earshot.

"Hey, honey. When are—?" Long pause. "No." Short pause. "No, I didn't. Clementine didn't sleep well—" Frustration mounted in her voice. Longer pause. "No. None of it's done. And where *are* you, a bar?"

Okey dokey then. I didn't like the turn this conversation had taken. Tired mom-of-many solo parenting during the run-up to Christmas plus exhausted traveling dad stranded out of town equaled marital distress. Didn't need to be a psychologist to see that.

Mom slipped through the door to the mudroom, closing it behind her.

I gave the noodles another stir, letting the steam warm my face, then pulled the aluminum colander from the cupboard and strategically positioned it over the mound of lunch dishes in the sink. A pot of sauce simmered on a rear stovetop burner, and I gave that a stir too, releasing the aroma of garlic and tomatoes. A peek inside the oven revealed some dinner rolls warming. The yeasty, buttery aroma triggered a growl from my empty stomach.

Mom emerged from the mudroom with Linus now asleep, his head against her shoulder, his little mouth open. The urge to touch his fuzzy little head grew too strong, so I gave it a rub and rose on tiptoes to press a kiss to his cheek.

Mom wiped an eye with the back of her hand. Had she been crying? No tell-tale red eyes or splotchy cheeks, but her somber expression made me think Dad had upset her.

"You okay, Mom?" I gave the boiling water a last swirl and set the spoon on the counter.

She gave me a sad smile. "I'm fine. Just . . . " She sighed. "I know this isn't the perfect Christmas you'd hoped for. And now, so much is unfinished . . . " She glanced around the kitchen where dishes mounted, recipe books lay open, and remnants of someone's lunch lay strewn over the countertop. "It's not even the slapdash Christmas I thought we could pull off."

My heart sank at her admission. This Christmas was a

bust. Even my mom, with her eternal optimism and low expectations couldn't deny it.

Christmas Eve morn, the delicious aroma of coffee brewing lured me downstairs earlier than I may have otherwise ventured out of my room. I didn't drink anything but the palest cappuccino, but I loved the smell of the real thing. Lily remained sleeping, but as my bare foot hit the cool tile at the bottom of the steps, I spied the other kids in the living room. Peter played a game on the electronic tablet, Clementine watched him, and Linus snoozed in his bouncy seat. My old bouncy seat, technically. Poor kid lived in, on, and with hand-me-down everything.

I found Mom in the kitchen, her natural habitat, cracking eggs into a bowl. Her hair, which had been acquiring gray strands around her temple and the jagged part on her left, was swept into a messy ponytail. She glanced up from the countertop when I entered the room. "Good morning. Sleep well?"

Shrugging, I snatched a crumb of cinnamon-raisin toast from a napkin-lined basket warming on the stovetop. "I guess so." A cursory glance around the room turned up no evidence of Dad's homecoming. "Did Dad make it home last night?"

A smile lit Mom's face. "He did. Around one in the morning." She glanced at the clock on the microwave oven. "We'll wake him up when breakfast is ready."

I reached for another scrap of toast then pulled back a

split second before Mom smacked my hand with her vinyl spatula. "Hey!"

Mom grinned. "Stop snitchin.'" She stirred the bowl of eggs with a whisk and sighed. "I've resigned myself to the fact that a lot of Christmas stuff isn't going to happen this year. Not with it being Christmas Eve already."

"Yeah, I figured." A decent night's sleep had given me some perspective. Was I still bummed that a random person could walk into our house this morning and never guess we were Christian for lack of any tangible sign of Christmas? (Okay, there was still that empty box of chocolate-covered cherries on the dining room floor, and it had some holly leaves and a red bow on it, but that totally didn't count. I bet even hardcore atheists ate Christmas candy.) Yes, I was bummed, but it didn't signal the coming of the apocalypse.

It meant I was the eldest child in the poster family for disorganized slackers. It meant a boring stretch of days that lacked the frivolity and *je ne sais* whatever that made Christmas magical, but I'd just have to deal. Surely we could salvage *something* of Christmas. I'd seen the spiral ham in the fridge, so it wouldn't be a total bust. *Baby Jesus will still be in the manger*, Mom would say. True statement, I knew, but in the back of my mind the thought niggled that Jesus wouldn't—*shouldn't*—bother with a family who couldn't honor Him by doing up His birthday right.

Squeals and a rumble of laughter from the next room told me Dad had woken.

In the living room, Dad, unshaven and wearing an

undershirt and blue flannel sleep pants, held Clementine in one arm while hugging Peter to his side. "Are you feeling better, sweetie?" he said, nuzzling Clementine's wispy blonde hair.

"Uh-huh," she said, then bark-coughed in his face.

Dad turned away, his face wrinkled in disgust, and spotted me. "Marigold, you look taller. I think you grew an inch while I was gone."

Unlikely. A glance in the mirror this morning told me I was still what my grandfather called pint-sized. "You think so?"

He released Peter and set Clementine on the floor, then opened his arms to me.

My heart fluttered in my chest as I crossed the room to him.

Dad's arms tightened around me, and his beard stubble grazed my temple. He smelled fresh and familiar.

I imagined myself fifty years in the future, sniffing an open jar of the facial scrub he used, recalling my dad. I hoped they never stopped making the stuff.

"You been helping your mom?" Dad mumbled into my hair.

A pang of guilt slashed across my heart. I'd changed Clementine a few times and helped the kids get ready for bed, but had I given Mom the help she needed? "Some."

He pulled back, holding me in front of him, a hand on each shoulder. "Some?" He lifted a brow in question.

"I could've done more I guess."

"Breakfast is ready!" Mom called from the kitchen.

Linus stirred, and Dad scooped him up and pressed kisses to his peach fuzz head on the way to the kitchen.

Over eggs, sliced fruit, and a pile of toast, Dad told us about his trip, the snow, the airport, and how glad he was to be home. Mom seemed unusually quiet though she smiled and spoke at all the appropriate times.

After the little ones had cleared their places to the best of their ability and Mom took Linus to nurse him in the living room, only Dad and I remained in the kitchen.

"Mom said you're not too happy about the lack of Christmas cheer around here." Dad leaned against the refrigerator and folded his arms across his chest. Ordinarily, the muscles in his arms weren't noticeable, but in this position, they stood out. A little paunch had grown around his middle though.

I snapped on Mom's green dishwashing gloves and dropped a handful of silverware into the sink. Hearing my childish complaint repeated back embarrassed me. Instead of making lists of more things for Mom to do, I should've been more help. "It's just . . . " I glanced at the doorway to the living room, where the *Paw Patrol* theme rang out. Lily must've finally woken up.

"It's just that we don't even have a tree up. Or lights outside. Or decorations." Should I name all of the ways in which we were unprepared? "And there're no cookies."

"No cookies?" Dad said, his voice and expression mocking but playful. "I'll have to flog your mom for that offense."

I grinned but turned my attention to the sink and ran

the hot water. "Go ahead, tell me I'm being selfish."

Dad unfolded his arms and moved closer, then pushed aside my hair and squeezed my shoulder. "You're not selfish for wanting the traditions you've come to expect. The things that help us keep Christmas special." He squeezed again and let go. "But you have to understand we have a new baby in the house, I've been gone—"

"I know, I know," I said, forcing back tears that had arisen from nowhere. A silly child, that's what I was.

"Listen, I didn't tell Mom yet, but Mr. Esposito texted me this morning and invited us to come over tonight. You know they'll have decorations galore." He nudged me with his elbow. "And *lots* of cookies. Wanna go?"

Maybe this Christmas could be salvaged after all. We'd just glom on to the Espositos' celebration. My old Halloween tormentor, Benny, and his family went all out for holidays. They had a big Christmas Eve party every year, and I think they always invited us, but we typically did our own thing.

I bounced on my toes. "That sounds awesome, Dad! Let's go!"

The Esposito household ran like a well-oiled machine. Outdoor decorations went up and down at the appropriate times. Stair-step children showed up on time—with matching socks and shoes no less—clean-faced and well-dressed at homeschool co-op and Sunday Mass. To-go cartons and pizza boxes never darkened the door of their home. Any room in their house would pass a white glove test. (Apparently their dust bunnies migrated to our house to die.) And their annual All Saints Day party was legendary.

"And how about being my date for Midnight Mass?" Dad's hazel eyes twinkled.

"Seriously? Yes, thank you, Dad." I flung my arms around Dad, knocking him backwards, and kissed his cheek.

He hugged me back, chuckling. "I'm looking forward to it." He released me and grabbed a coffee mug from the cabinet. "But first, we've got a tree to put up."

By late afternoon, Dad, Peter, and I had assembled and decorated the tree. Our shabby angel, Angie, sat ramrod straight atop the tree, skimming the ceiling. Garlands made of pine cones and red fabric bows draped the boughs, and an assortment of ornaments dangled from the tips of the artificial limbs—red satin balls, plastic-bead icicles, and ornaments my parents made when they were kids. All of the breakable items had been strategically placed out of reach of Lily and Clementine.

Multi-colored lights glimmering, the tree stood in front of the living room picture window. *Majestic.*

Outside, Peter steadied the ladder, and I fed Dad strands of lights that he wrapped around the porch pillars and railings. Dad tossed a net-style set of lights over the fat boxwood bush along the driveway, I hung an old wreath on the front door, and we called it a day.

Inside, Mom had managed to pull a couple of boxes of decorations from the attic. The boxes sat, lids open and contents strewn on the coffee table, while she fed Linus.

Dad, Peter, and I hung our coats on the rack as Lily descended the steps, a small department store gift box in her hands. On the top, in black magic marker, it read "Nativity." A wide grinned stretched across her cheeks.

Her foot, hidden somewhere in a puffy royal blue slipper with a giant *Paw Patrol* pup head, caught on one of the dinosaurs I'd knocked over yesterday. She yelped and grabbed for the rail, sending the box tumbling down the steps.

I stretched a hand out, hoping to grab the box before impact, but it landed upside down on the tile floor.

My spine tensed at the sound of something shattering.

Seeing ceramic shards spilling onto the floor, Peter gasped and clapped a hand over his mouth.

Lily, who seemed no worse physically for her misadventure, wailed at the sight on the entryway floor. Alongside the overturned box lid, two camels, covered in regal blankets, lay decapitated. An angel had lost her wings, and baby Jesus lay face down beside it.

I stooped and picked up the tiny statue of my Savior, afraid of what I might find. I examined it, careful not to do any more damage. One skinned knee, a scraped nose, and only one hand.

Dad bit out a swear word, and Mom didn't bother to scold him.

So much for setting up the crèche.

After a shower, I dressed in a black turtleneck, a red

plaid tartan skirt, and black suede knee-high boots since Mom hadn't gotten to repairing my dress. With my hair in an attempt at a sophisticated updo, I felt mature and cultured. No one would guess my tights sported cartoon narwhals below the knees.

Mom and Dad's conversation drifted from their room across the hall.

"I want to go, but with Clementine coughing, I think we're better off here. And I have a better shot of getting Peter and Lily to bed at a decent hour, even if Linus is wide awake." Mom sounded both disappointed and relieved, which seemed about right. "It'll be good for Marigold, too, to have one of us to herself for a change."

"Yeah, but I just got back and now I'm leaving," Dad said, then murmured something I couldn't make out. A stretch of silence made me think they were kissing — something that I did *not* want to imagine. They weren't prone to displays of affection, even in front of us kids, but considering their obvious efforts to keep the United States birth rate at or above replacement level, the romance mustn't have been dead.

I stepped into the hall, keeping them out of my line of sight, cleared my throat loudly, and knocked on the wooden trim of their open bedroom door. "I'm ready, Dad."

After a couple of beats during which I stared at the darkness beyond the hall window, Dad emerged wearing an olive-colored button down shirt and a pair of khaki pants. His face was clean shaven, and he'd applied some gel to his hair, which was peppered with a lot more gray than Mom's.

"Don't you look pretty," Dad said, extending his arm for me to take.

My cheeks warmed, and I relished his compliment. For the first time, I wondered what other teenagers might be at this Esposito shindig. Benny, obviously, but maybe he had some cousins our age. Or maybe some other kids from co-op would be there.

The homeschool co-op group had shrunk over the past four months with one family transitioning their kids to public school, one opting for cyberschool, and two others moving, including my best friend Regina's family.

Worst case scenario, I stayed glued to Dad's side.

Bundled in coats and gloves, Dad and I hugged and kissed everyone goodbye, wishing them a merry Christmas since we wouldn't be back until late.

Outside, frigid air, much colder than when we'd hung the lights this afternoon, nipped my nose and ears.

I shoved my gloved hands into my pockets as we strode across the yard and onto the wooded trail that would take us through a couple of undeveloped lots and to the Espositos.

Dad used his cell phone to light the path, which we kids traversed daily during summer, on foot and on bicycles. Semi-frozen dead leaves crunched beneath our feet, but otherwise, the woods remained still, not betraying the presence of the squirrels, deer, and other creatures I knew lived there.

A cloud shifted, and soft moonlight bathed the Espositos' yard as we emerged from the woods into the meadow that marked their property line. Next to a gnarly apple tree, the aluminum roof of the kids' pressed-board summer shack glinted in the moonlight.

As we crossed the sprawling lawn, warm light shone from every window of the Esposito's imposing residence. White lights flashed in an erratic rhythm along the gutters on the first and second floors. On the front lawn, the same white lights adorned several trees and lit an old-fashioned sleigh that held a couple of fancy presents wrapped in gold paper and giant red bows. Flurries fell from the sky, first a smattering, and then so many that in a few short minutes, a squall chased us to the front door.

The swirling flakes made me feel as if I'd landed in a snow globe. And if Dad weren't with me, I'd have spun around, catching snowflakes on my tongue until I collapsed in a dizzy heap on the cold ground.

Dad pressed the doorbell as we huddled together, anxious to get inside.

After a moment, the door swung open. A pleasant aroma came from within the house, a delectable mixture of savory and sweet. Mr. Esposito stood in the entry way, a drink in his hand and a smile on his face. "Joel, Marigold, come on in!"

"Merry Christmas, Bill," Dad said, ushering me in ahead of him.

"Where's Carla and the rest of the gang?" He peered outside, as if we'd lost them in the snowstorm.

Dad explained about Clementine's croup and Mom staying home with the kids, while we handed Mr. Esposito our coats.

His office sat to the right of the entryway, and he stacked our coats atop a mound of others on his desk. "It's really coming down out there. They're saying we might get four to five inches."

"I guess it's arriving earlier than they expected." Dad rubbed at his arms as if he were warming himself. "Hey," he said, nodding at Mr. Esposito's drink, "can I get one of those?"

"Sure thing." He turned his gaze to me. "Make yourself at home. Food's almost ready in the dining room. Drinks are in the kitchen. The little kids are upstairs and the older kids are in the basement." He glanced down the hall. "Benny's lurking around here somewhere."

I nodded and bit down on a smile. Benny was a quiet guy, but I hadn't pegged him as a lurker. Except for his role in the aforementioned Halloween incident that had scarred me for life.

Mrs. Esposito bustled towards us, arms outstretched in welcome. From her perfectly styled hair and her flawless makeup, all the way down to her bedazzled stilettos, she communicated competence and poise.

I wouldn't say my mom dressed like a frump, but if it were the '90s, she'd be rocking the homeschool mom denim jumper. "Dowdy" came to mind as an apt description of her everyday look. My mom simply didn't care about fashion.

"Marigold, what a lovely young woman you've become!" Mrs. Esposito looked me up and down approvingly.

My chest swelled under her praise. "Thank you."

I glanced around the foyer, where large red balls and gold stars hung suspended from the ceiling, glittering in the light of a half-dozen large pillar candles. Beside the candles, a spray of red berries and evergreen leaves in a holiday arrangement sprung from a large urn on a wooden console table.

Mr. and Mrs. Esposito accompanied Dad to their makeshift bar in the kitchen while I hung back in the dining room. At the end of the long table, stacks of ruby red chargers lay next to gold-trimmed ivory plates and silverware rolled in pine green linen napkins. A large, flickering candle arrangement sat in the center of the elegant table runner.

Serving platters filled with seafood covered the rest of the table. My idea of seafood was breaded flounder or popcorn shrimp, but this elegant spread included salmon, oysters, lobster, scallops, crab, and more.

I began to feel a bit like a fish myself—a fish out of water.

Wondering where everyone was, I circled round the table then ambled to the living room, where the scent of fresh pine greeted me. In one corner, a live tree at least eight-feet tall stood adorned with sparkly blue and silver ornaments.

How did they keep their little kids from destroying

such a magnificent tree? In our house, it'd be trashed in seconds flat.

Next to the tree, on an oval table, a three-tiered silver cookie stand displayed an endless variety of homemade sweet treats—some chocolate, some covered in powdered sugar, and others in mini foil baking cups. Nearby, adults stood in clusters of three or four, talking and laughing.

In the opposite corner, on a plush, high-backed chair, Benny sat, his head bent over a book. Finally, someone I knew!

He glanced up as I approached, careful to keep his place in the book with his hand. Benny's bright orange hair always stood on end, which had earned him the nickname Beaker. Like the shy lab assistant from *The Muppet Show*, who only said "meep." The glasses he'd gotten last summer only emphasized the awkward nerd vibe he had going, but he'd always been a likable kid, the kind who never cheated or bullied, the kind adults loved 'cause he was so polite. (Again, the Halloween incident notwithstanding.)

He stood, looking a lot taller than when I'd last seen him, and extended a gangly arm to me. "Merry Christmas," he said. "I didn't know your family was coming this year."

Mirroring his good manners, I accepted his hand and shook it. "Just me and my dad," I said.

We chatted for a few minutes about co-op and the weather, and then he returned to his book. What book was engrossing enough to keep you from socializing at your own Christmas party? I could think of a few, but I doubted Benny read inspirational romances.

I passed the next few hours mainly at Dad's side, occasionally venturing up or down the stairs where the little and big kids congregated. Benny and I talked a few more times. And I ate more seafood than I had in the past five years combined. Plus a few cookies.

The imposing grandfather clock beside the mantel chimed, signaling eleven o'clock.

I nudged Dad during a break in the conversation. "Shouldn't we get going to Mass?"

He turned his gaze toward me, his mouth turned down. "Aw, honey. Have you looked outside? I don't think Midnight Mass is a good idea tonight. We'll wait and go in the morning with the rest of the family. They'll have the roads cleared by then."

Before I could protest, he'd returned to his conversation.

My fists clenched tight, and I ground my teeth, forcing myself to move in a normal gait and not stomp. Seething and hurt, I sought the nearest window. The inside light made it difficult to see outside, so I leaned against the glass and cupped my hands around my eyes.

To my surprise, at least five inches of snow covered the lawn, the landscaping, and the Christmas sleigh.

I'd gotten my white Christmas. *Thanks, God.*

Thinking of the hills, valleys, and hairpin turns in the coal region where we lived, I had to admit Dad's decision seemed prudent, but it did little to diminish my disappointment.

I'd half turned from the window when a bright light from outside caught my attention, drawing my gaze to the Espositos' driveway.

A large, school-bus sized recreational vehicle bumped over the curb and into the driveway, its windshield wipers pushing snow from the windows. The behemoth vehicle stopped, and an air horn sounded.

Inside, all heads turned toward the windows in the front of the house. Mr. and Mrs. Esposito crossed the living room toward the front door, while outside, the RV doors opened.

A stocky man descended the passenger side steps, followed by two others—maybe a teen and definitely a little girl, based on the dress she wore. Another man rounded the front of the vehicle, and the four of them shuffled through the snow-covered walk toward the front porch.

People resumed their conversations.

Now that we weren't going to Mass, I was eager to go home. I'd exhausted all topics of interest with Benny, and I hadn't gotten past small talk with anyone else, young or old. I crossed the room to Dad and tugged on his sleeve.

Loud, angry voices came from the foyer, again drawing all the guests' attention. I made out a smattering of sentences, including Mrs. Esposito asking, "Where's Joy?" in a shrill tone.

Someone bumped me from behind, scattering my thoughts and hampering my ability to decipher the ongoing conversation, which steadily grew louder and

more strained.

"Sorry," Benny muttered, squeezing behind me. "My Uncle Steve and my cousins are here," he said, his eyes never meeting mine.

Dad and I exchanged a look. *Want to go home?* he seemed to say.

"I'm ready," I said aloud.

Dad said his goodbyes, and we made our way to the foyer, where tension ripped through the air. Voices had quieted, but Uncle Steve and company stood opposite Benny's parents, and nothing about the encounter seemed merry or bright.

I nodded to Benny as we slipped by and grabbed our coats from Mr. Esposito's office.

Outside, only flurries drifted from the near-midnight sky, and the thick blanket of snow lit the return path through the woods.

Wishing I'd worn snow boots instead of my more fashionable suede boots, I held tight to Dad's arm, shivering.

Neither of us spoke much on the way back. Maybe the awkward end to the evening kept us quiet. As a guest, I'd never felt more like an intruder. For all the splendor of the Espositos' Christmas Eve celebration, apparently perfection had eluded them too.

Dad asked me if I'd had a good time and whether Benny and I were friends. He pointed out how the icy snow covering the tree limbs glinted in the moonlight, reminding him of the mental image he'd drawn of Narnia.

We reached our yard, and I scampered to the door, my toes cold and wet.

Once inside, Dad shut and bolted the door behind us.

The horrible stench of vomit greeted us.

I covered my nose and mouth with my hand. "Do you smell that?" I said, my words smothered by my palm.

Dad nodded, his face scrunched in revulsion.

As I hung up my coat, I noticed the tree still lit in the living room. Opposite it, Mom sat on the couch, gazing at it as flashes of red and green lit her face.

Dad passed me, went to Mom, and kissed her on the forehead. He said something I couldn't hear, they exchanged a few words and a couple of Christmas wishes, and then he retreated to the upstairs, patting my arm on his way.

Mom, wearing a long flannel nightgown and fuzzy socks, smiled at me. "How was it?"

I kicked off my wet suede boots and joined her in the living room, where it didn't smell so putrid. "Good, I guess." I shrugged. "I hung out with Dad or Benny, ate a lot of seafood. Then it got real awkward at the end when Benny's uncle got there."

Mom nodded. "Dad mentioned it."

"Who got sick?" I needed to know so I could mentally retrace the day and assess my risk of contracting the dreaded bug based on the amount of contact I'd had with patient zero. Or recall, God forbid, whether I'd eaten from his or her leftovers.

"Peter, a couple of hours ago." Mom sighed. "At least

he went right back to sleep."

We'd decorated outdoors together, but otherwise, I hadn't been too close to Peter. Bullet dodged—at least I hoped.

Mom gestured toward a round, open tin on the end table. "I made some buckeyes for us."

My eyes widened. Buckeye candies in all their peanut buttery, chocolate goodness were my favorite. I was sorry I didn't get to help make them, but that wouldn't stop me from enjoying them.

I reached for one and froze. "Did Peter help make these?"

Mom chuckled. "No. I made them myself."

I popped one in my mouth and groaned. "These are delicious," I said around a mouthful of peanut butter.

On the couch arm, a glimmer of silver caught my eye—the silver stitching on my Christmas dress. With the dress lying face down, the zipper showed, newly sewn into place and fully functional. *Oh, Mom. You didn't forget.* My heart swelled with gratitude.

Taking a seat close to Mom, I rested my head against her shoulder and admired the tree. We'd done a good job. In the dim room, though the Espositos' tree dwarfed ours in both size and quality, I kinda loved its simplicity.

On the tree skirt, someone had attempted to re-assemble our nativity. One camel sat, accompanied by two My Little Pony figures—Rainbow Dash and Shutterfly, by the looks of it. Masking tape held the angel's wings in place where she dangled by an open paper clip from a low-hanging branch. The oxen and sheep grazed alongside a shepherd boy and the Magi, who were way too close to the scene. We had a couple weeks until the Epiphany, after all.

In the center, Mary and Joseph knelt on either side of the manger. And in the center lay baby Jesus, a small Band-Aid affixed to his wrist and stretched across his body.

I didn't know whether to laugh or cry.

Tears swelled in my eyes, and my heart sank a bit as I thought about how our Christmas wouldn't be all that I'd hoped for. We'd missed Midnight Mass, Peter and Clementine were sick, and we had only the buckeyes to nosh.

My heart warmed, and I blinked away the unshed tears that made the Christmas lights form starbursts. I had a lot to be thankful for. Dad had made it home, we'd thrown together the tree and some decorations, and we had an adorable little miracle with the unfortunate name of a Peanuts characters.

In comparison, the Espositos' Christmas *looked* picture perfect, and I'd thought it was, with their gorgeous home, their fancy dinner, and all of their expensive Christmas trappings.

But the hubbub in the foyer showed my perception had been wrong.

I studied the plastic-bandaged baby Jesus. His hand-painted blue eyes still welcomed. His outstretched arms still beckoned. The twinkling lights dangling above Him created a heavenly aura that stirred my soul.

Maybe Jesus didn't come *despite* my imperfect life. Or the Espositos' imperfect life.

Maybe Jesus came *because* of it.

Maybe our imperfect lives, our desperate need for a Savior, made us perfect *in Him*.

If I approached my Lord and Savior on the back of a dirty, bedraggled My Little Pony with a twisted mane and knotted tail, the air smelling like sick, and I was too distracted to recognize all my blessings, He'd still welcome me. He'd hold me fast to Him, "God with us"— Emmanuel.

*_**_**

If you'd like to get better acquainted with Marigold, Benny, and their brush with danger in a burning ghost town, look for a full-length novel about them slated for a 2021 release, God-willing!

ABOUT THE AUTHOR

CAROLYN ASTFALK writes from the sweetest place on Earth, Hershey, Pennsylvania, where she lives with her husband and four children. In addition to her contemporary Catholic romances (sometimes referred to as Theology of the Body fiction), including the young adult coming-of-age story *Rightfully Ours*, she writes for CatholicMom.com and *Today's Catholic Teacher*. When she's not washing dishes, doing laundry, or reading, you can find her blogging about books, family life, and faith at www.CarolynAstfalk.com.

OPERATION GIFT DROP

by Theresa Linden

In the not-so-distant future, unbeknownst to the all-controlling government, a group of rebels deep underground watch over the city of Aldonia. In order to rescue the few who refuse to fall in step with the government's bad ideologies, who cannot fit in, who long for true freedom, they train and prepare. They are the Mosheh.

"Move out." Dedrick's rough, commanding voice came from a distance.

Seventeen-year-old Bolcan dropped the last of his opponents to the ground with his signature sleeper hold and stooped over to catch his breath. Sweat dripped from a lock of Bolcan's golden hair and into his eyes, stinging and blurring the view of Dedrick's dark, stealthy form against the evening sky and the buildings around them.

Anxious to complete this mission, Bolcan jogged toward Dedrick. His heart raced with the impossible speed that only came from a rush of adrenaline. He'd enjoyed the hand-to-hand fight against four burly men—even though they were only 3D foes in a virtual reality environment. The sensors and devices on his body had made it feel freakishly real . . . especially if he compared it to the full-on fight that had gotten him thrown out of Secondary for the last time. And sent to Re-Education for the last time too.

Man, he was thankful the Mosheh had rescued him a year ago. And that today he was training to rescue others.

Bolcan slowed as he drew near.

"Gotta switch gears and take it down a notch, Bolcan. Remember the mission." Dedrick Ryder, an athletic dude in a black t-shirt and urban camouflage trousers, was one of the Mosheh's youngest trainers.

"Do you always leave your comrades hanging when they've been ambushed?" Stopping two meters away, Bolcan brushed his shoulder-length hair off his neck then clenched a fist to emphasize his muscles. Sure, Dedrick was the trainer and testing Bolcan's choices and moves, but he could've given a hand in the fight.

"I took care of the last two that you didn't even notice." Dedrick walked backwards as he spoke. "Besides, it depends on the comrade and the trouble he leaves behind." He turned and jogged toward their destination, a three-story manufacturing building.

Bolcan kept pace with him. "Trouble? So I knocked over a pedestrian. Big deal." Just before the ambush, the instant their destination had come into view, Bolcan's legs had itched to sprint the last four hundred or so meters, but a long line of people blocked his path. Creeping along at a snail's pace, most walked down the sidewalk by twos and left little space for a person to get through. He'd had no choice but to break the line.

"That pedestrian was an old lady. Most of them were old. Didn't you see a few had canes? Probably all live at the senior center, out taking a walk, and you just plowed through them."

"Out taking a walk . . . " Bolcan laughed. "How often does that happen? Once they move in, they rarely leave the place."

"They left the place today."

"This is *virtual* reality, Dedrick. I've noticed that you take these training games too seriously." Granted, Dedrick was a colony boy so he hadn't grown up with 3D games, probably never played electronic games at all until he joined the Mosheh, and they did look real. As an Aldonian, Bolcan had played them practically since birth. The technology was no big deal to him. He knew what he could get away with in a game. Some obstacles were silly, others serious challenges.

Slowing as they neared the building, Dedrick gritted his teeth. Typically self-possessed, maybe his impulsive and overly-sensitive response to the situation embarrassed him. Once Bolcan had blown through the line of pedestrians, a few shrieks and a shout in his wake, Dedrick had run to an old woman's aid—a computer-generated woman who had nothing to do with their training mission. He should've kept up with Bolcan. If Bolcan and Dedrick had been together, maybe those four dudes would've thought twice about an ambush.

"All right. Well, we're running out of time." Dedrick motioned Bolcan closer and then checked the scenario-monitoring device clipped to his belt.

Curious, Bolcan tried to glimpse the device too. Dedrick would see Bolcan's ratings for the combat portion of the exercise. He'd been running training operations for new Mosheh members all week. Maybe Bolcan's ratings would impress him. Or . . . more likely, he was just gathering details for the next stage of the exercise.

How'd a mere twenty-year-old get that role anyway? Well, if Dedrick could do it—a kid nowhere near as muscular and capable as Bolcan—Bolcan could do it too. Maybe in a couple of years, he'd be training the new Mosheh members.

A cool breeze kicked up, refreshing Bolcan's clammy skin while he sized up the three-story building before them. They needed to get inside and up to the third floor to leave a message for a certain dude ASAP, and Dedrick had left it up to Bolcan to get the job done.

"Door's locked," Dedrick said, though Bolcan hadn't seen him try the knob.

"It's late. The windows are dark. I'm sure no one's inside. We wouldn't be sent on a mission during operating hours, would we?"

Dedrick shrugged. "Sometimes. Not everything is done in stealth mode. It's not always necessary."

"Yeah, well, as long as someone like *you* didn't design this training program, I'm sure no one is here."

Dedrick shrugged again, his expression neutral as if

Bolcan's insult had simply rolled off him. He must've known this training exercise by heart, but he wouldn't want to give anything away.

Grabbing the metal knob—his gaming gloves making it feel cold and solid—Bolcan found Dedrick's assessment true. It was locked. Then he checked the contents of his virtual backpack: large box, water bottle, medical kit, hatchet, pistol, lockpick . . .

He reached for the lockpick but then grabbed the hatchet and pistol instead. He hadn't mastered using a lockpick yet and doubted he had the time to waste. But he could swing a hatchet.

Dedrick backed up.

Bolcan handed him the pistol, assuming he would cover Bolcan if necessary. Without giving it a second thought, he swung hard, cracking the blunt end of the hatchet against the doorknob. A few swings later, the knob hung askew and the door cracked open.

Proud of himself, Bolcan laughed and made a move to push it open further with his shoulder, but the door swung freely and he lost his balance, falling into a foyer. Angry figures came from doorways and a cacophony of shouting surrounded him. His knee cracked down on the hard floor.

Then everything and everyone froze in place, and Dedrick's sigh replaced the shouting.

"Look, Bolcan, not every problem is solved with brute force." Dedrick grabbed Bolcan's upper arm and yanked him backward and to his feet. "See this box in your inventory?"

Bolcan shook the hair off his forehead and glanced. "Yeah, so?"

"So"—Dedrick locked his steady brown eyes onto Bolcan's—"we knock on the door first. And, yes, people are here. Then we easily gain entrance by saying we're delivering this package to our man. The Mosheh does not regard everyone as an enemy. We don't want to hurt anyone if we don't have to. We don't destroy things without good cause. To succeed as one of us, you need humility."

One week later, 2:00 a.m. December 25th in the underground Mosheh facility . . .

"You heading for the control center?" A dark-haired girl caught Bolcan at the foot of the wide ramp leading to the expansive Mosheh Control Center. Without waiting for his answer, she handed him a big plastic bag. "Give this to Miriam, huh?" She beamed a smile and took off.

Her good mood elevating his even more, he slung the lightweight bag—felt like a load of laundry—over his shoulder and continued up the ramp to the center. Groups of kids near glowing screens and workstations spoke over one another in excited voices. Laughter echoed in the open area that stretched out to darkness on either side. Joy and anticipation had been mounting all day. And now that the elders had retired for the night, the younger Mosheh members were gathering for an annual excursion called Operation Gift Drop.

Bolcan had tried to get someone to explain this operation to him, but he'd only gotten answers like "Come and see," "It's a tradition," and "You'll love it." The indoctrination and re-education he'd known over the years as a citizen of Aldonia had left him empty and hungry for something real and deep, so he appreciated these people with their organic history, heartfelt dedication, and meaningful traditions. And he was glad they allowed Aldonians to join them.

Halfway through the control center, he spotted Miriam, the only person over forty who hadn't retired for the night, as far as he'd noticed. She stood near several waist-high crates, talking to a kid whose tense gestures made him seem like the only one with a negative attitude tonight.

Wait—She was talking to Dedrick Ryder. He stood with his back to Bolcan. Neither seemed to notice Bolcan approach, and he soon made out their conversation.

"So let him do something inside. He can help disrupt the surveillance. That's an important job," Dedrick said. "He's not ready to go out."

"Look, Dedrick, this isn't a dangerous rescue mission. It's just a bit of fun." Miriam playfully shoved Dedrick's arm, the one he'd been waving as he spoke.

"There are still risks and he's too—"

Miriam's eyes shifted to Bolcan and a genuine smile stretched across her face. She wore her hair in a ponytail, a few gray strands showing on the sides, and a fuzzy red sweater—not her usual attire at all. Bolcan had only seen her in somber colors or camouflage.

"You talking about me? I'm too what?"

Dedrick glanced over his shoulder and then turned toward Bolcan with a sneer. "Oh, hey. Didn't know you were eavesdropping."

"You don't think I'm ready because you've never really tested me one-on-one. We only do those lame simulations." He wanted to say more. Either he needed a new trainer or Dedrick needed to lighten up. Dedrick was one of many trainers, not the one in charge of formation. And as a trainer, he was too rigid—cautious, judgmental, something of a perfectionist—more like one of the elders even at his young age. He had no idea what it was like to grow up in Aldonia. And he knew nothing of Bolcan's abilities.

"Those lame simulations tell me more about your readiness than you'd guess."

"Oh, I'm ready. You can try me right now." Conscious of their difference in size, Bolcan grinned and flexed a bicep.

Dedrick held Bolcan's gaze for a second then glanced at the darkness overhead and shook his head, a smile spreading across his face.

Putting his irritation in check, Bolcan swung the bag off his shoulder and offered it to Miriam. "I was told to give this to you."

"Oh, thanks." Her face lit up. She set the bag in an open crate—on more bags, these ones made of weathered canvas and stuffed with lumpy contents. "Here, Dedrick, put this on." From the bag Bolcan had brought her, she drew out a red cloth hat with fluffy white trim and a pompom on the pointy end.

Dedrick finally smiled, and he did nothing to stop Miriam from arranging the silly thing on his head.

"You too," she said to Bolcan, producing a second hat from the bag.

"Oh, we need a picture!" Camilla, the ever-cheerful colony girl, bounced up as Miriam pulled the bright red hat down over Bolcan's ears and arranged a lock of his shoulder-length golden hair. She grabbed Dedrick by the arms and positioned him next to Bolcan, Dedrick's eyes rolling the whole time, though he continued to smile.

Bolcan threw his arm around Dedrick's shoulders for the shot and grinned as big as he could, as if they were best friends and not rivals.

"Better not let an elder see the pics," a kid said in passing.

"Now you two need one of these." Miriam shoved a big, loaded canvas bag between Dedrick and Bolcan. "And if you hurry, you'll catch the next tunnel kart."

Eyes on Miriam, Dedrick stepped back and lifted his hands. "If he's coming along, he can carry it." He strode toward the tunnel entrance.

Glad that Miriam hadn't changed her mind because of Dedrick's counsel, Bolcan grabbed the bag and took off after Dedrick. He'd prove himself to Dedrick one way or another tonight.

"What's so different about this mission that the elders can't know?" With the heavy sack slung over one shoulder, Bolcan walked alongside Dedrick. "You trainers have always pounded it into us that we are to honor, obey, and respect the elders, and to trust in their wisdom over our own. Now we're sneaking around without the elders' permission."

The beam of Dedrick's flashlight lit up their concrete path. High walls rose up on either side, gradually getting lower the further they walked through the tunnel. Laughter, voices, and a few points of light came from ahead.

"It's a tradition that goes back to the beginnings of the Mosheh." Dedrick glanced at Bolcan, his look less rigid now. "The younger members carry out this assignment in secrecy." A smile made its way to his face. "I don't doubt the elders know all about it, but this night we go out without permission. Don't get me wrong—obedience to the elders is essential, but Operation Gift Drop reminds us that God is our highest authority and serving Him our highest goal."

Bolcan nodded as if it now made sense, though he'd need to think on it another time. Aldonia's all-controlling government, the Regimen Custodia Terra, had always taught about the earth as if it were the highest good, a goddess not only to be protected and cared for but almost worshipped. Humans, left to themselves, were akin to parasites. Those teachings had never sat right with him, but he could not grasp the idea of a god as the colonists saw it either.

The colonists' God did not need to be protected. He

protected His people. And they worshipped Him, even without seeing Him. No, that was wrong. They did see Him. At every Mass. Bolcan had attended only once. The songs, bells, incense, and prayers in a strange language had stirred his soul with a longing for something great and wonderful. But when the priest had lifted high into the air a tiny, circular-shaped piece of bread and the person next to Bolcan said it was God, Bolcan had not understood. And he'd never gone back. What kind of God would make Himself so vulnerable and weak as to become food?

A few minutes later, Bolcan sat with one leg hanging off a tunnel kart, clinging to the back of a seat and smashed up against another kid. Six of them had piled onto a kart that seated four, three bulging canvas sacks precariously balanced or stuffed between bodies. The engine whined at a higher decibel with its extra load. Without warning, the kid next to Bolcan began a chant and the others joined in, repeating it about a dozen times. "Hail and blessed be the hour and the moment when the Son of God was born . . . "

Bolcan tried tuning it out. The repetition stirred up disturbing thoughts of Re-Ed, though the cheerful spirit of this group and their reverence while praying reminded him of nothing he'd known in Aldonia.

Ten minutes later found everyone but Bolcan singing jolly songs, one about snow and sleighs, and another about heaven and nature. He might've heard that one before, but the words were different, so he sang along inside his head. *Joy to the world, the time has come, let earth her bounty bring, let e-everyone prepare Her-r room, and earth and nature sing . . .*

Before long, they approached an intersection of dark tunnels and Dedrick hollered, "This is our stop."

As the kart squeaked to a halt, Bolcan jumped off, glad to stretch his legs. A faint gray light shone at some distance down the tunnel to the left, nothing to the right. He didn't know which way to go because Dedrick—probably hoping he wouldn't come along—hadn't prepared him for this mission.

"We've got a twenty-minute hike ahead of us. Through the tunnels." Dedrick gestured into the darkness, came around the back of the kart, and shoved the canvas bag at Bolcan.

Bolcan considered telling Dedrick to take a turn carrying the bag, and his expression may have communicated that, but he kept his mouth shut and swung the bag over his shoulder.

"Godspeed," Dedrick shouted to the others as he adjusted his droopy red hat. They responded with a few hoots and well wishes, and the driver took off down the tunnel with the distant light, heading toward the next drop-off point. Leaving Bolcan and Dedrick alone.

"What's our destination?" Bolcan asked.

"We'll hit one of the primary residences. It'll be a first for them." Dedrick glanced at him, the light of his flashlight revealing the hint of a smile. "I wish we could hit all of them, but Aldonia's too big and there aren't that many of us. We try to deliver to different places every year, different factories, government offices, retirement communities. Everywhere we can. Eventually, over the years, we'll hit them all."

Fifteen minutes later, a cramp in his arm and the rough canvas digging into his palm had Bolcan transferring the heavy bag to his other shoulder. "You ready to take a turn carrying this?"

"Huh?" Without slowing his stride, Dedrick studied the TekBand on his wrist. Not only a communication device, the TekBand provided an abundance of information that the rescuers needed—things like maps, stats, and direction. Bolcan had yet to be issued one. "Nah, we're almost there. You can handle it."

"I know I can." Attitude slipped out in Bolcan's tone. "I can handle a lot more than you give me credit for."

Dedrick merely glanced at him.

Bolcan's irritation grew at Dedrick's lack of response. "Any day you want to try me, I'll prove it."

"You're proving the opposite with comments like that."

"Oh yeah?" Taking Dedrick's reply as fighting words, Bolcan swung the bag to the cold concrete at his feet and raised his fists. "Why don't you test me right now? I'll have you immobilized within a couple of minutes, if that long. Then you carry the bag."

Dedrick took six more steps. He stopped and turned to face Bolcan, the beam of his flashlight hitting the floor between them. A tilt of his head and quirk of a grin on his shadowy face made him look amused, but his squinted eyes told otherwise. "You want to fight me right here?"

Realizing he still wore the silly red hat and imagining what he must look like, Bolcan yanked it off and tossed it.

"Right here. Right now. And when I win, you stop doubting my abilities. There's nothing you can do that I can't."

"Really, Bolcan, it's not about your ability to fight. I've been trying to tell you, there's more to it—"

"But you don't think I can beat you."

"I didn't say that."

"You say it with your attitude."

Dedrick shook his head and pressed his lips together—thinking it over or holding back a retort? Then he set his flashlight against the wall, leaving the beam to illuminate the floor, dropped his red hat beside it and shrugged out of his jacket. "Push the bag out of the way. I don't want any gifts ruined. First one to restrain the other wins. Loser carries the bag."

"Which you think will be me."

"Look, I just want to deliver gifts. You want to fight. So let's get this over with."

A bit surprised that Dedrick was agreeing to this fight but more than happy for this chance to prove himself, Bolcan shoved the bag next to the flashlight, pushed his hair behind his ears, and took a fighter's stance: elbows in, fists at cheek level, and chin tucked.

Dedrick staggered his feet and brought his hands up and open as if he really didn't want to do this. "There are better ways to prove yourself."

"At the moment, none come to mind." Bolcan swung first, aiming for Dedrick's jaw but hitting only air as Dedrick twisted and slapped Bolcan's arm aside with a look of disinterest on his face. Bolcan had seen Dedrick fight other Mosheh members in demonstrations. His moves were smooth and refined, but he'd never fought someone like Bolcan. Bolcan didn't need smooth moves; he could street fight.

Aiming for Dedrick's side and throwing his weight into the move, Bolcan swung.

Dedrick blocked the punch with his elbow and another twist, and then threw a body shot that hit its mark.

Exhaling sharply, Bolcan forced himself to ignore the jolt of pain in his abdomen and jumped back to avoid Dedrick's arm around his neck. Maybe Dedrick meant to end this in a few moves, but Bolcan wasn't having it. More thoughtful this time, Bolcan readied himself to make another attack. He didn't need a bunch of shots but only power behind a few good ones. A solid shot to the ribs could knock the wind out of Dedrick, then Bolcan could get him in a hold and claim victory. He feigned a throw to the head and went for Dedrick's side.

As if foreseeing it, Dedrick twisted, avoiding the headshot, and yanked Bolcan's other arm, throwing him off balance. Dedrick swung his arm toward Bolcan's throat and might've taken command right then, but Bolcan regained his balance, forced himself forward, and had Dedrick staggering back instead.

Now Dedrick was on his toes, throwing shots and dodging to avoid Bolcan's attacks, not acting so casual and disinterested as Bolcan took control of the space between them. Bouncing on the balls of his feet, maybe annoyed that he hadn't taken Bolcan down yet, he said, "We're wasting time here, Bolcan. This fight won't convince me of anything except that you're lacking in self-control and humility."

"Humility?" Bolcan's right hook met with Dedrick's palm.

Shaking his hand out, still bouncing on his feet, Dedrick said, "You're Aldonian, so that's a tough one," and he landed a low kick on Bolcan's shins.

Unwilling to react to the pain, Bolcan circled Dedrick and let loose a few rapid jabs, one or two successful. Then it happened. Dedrick wound up with his back to the wall, the canvas bag tangling his feet, and he tried to recover ground with a clinch. He wasn't prepared for Bolcan's muscular build, one he worked on every day while Dedrick wasted his time in the Mosheh Control Center or ventured out on rescue missions.

Gaining some distance from the wall, Dedrick tried to break the clinch, and Bolcan used that instant to come up beside Dedrick and get his arm around his neck. He was about to own Dedrick with a sleeper hold.

Dedrick latched onto Bolcan's arm but couldn't lessen the grip no matter how he tried. One second, two seconds, three . . . He must've known it was over—

To secure his position, Bolcan shifted his weight and took a step, but something caught his foot and . . . and wouldn't let go. That lousy canvas bag!

Thrown off balance, Bolcan stumbled to the side.

Taking advantage of the moment, Dedrick jerked

forward, took a wide stance and squatted, breaking Bolcan's hold. He swung a fist down and back, cracking Bolcan's knee.

A jolt of pain had Bolcan curling forward in agony. Then Dedrick's fist sailed over his shoulder and landed on Bolcan's nose.

Seeing stars but not giving up, Bolcan formed a fist and readied a swing. Before he could even think about executing a move, Dedrick spun to face him, grabbed his fist and elbow, and twisted, overextending Bolcan's shoulder and making him lose balance.

In the next instant—somehow—Dedrick slammed Bolcan down.

The air shot from Bolcan's lungs and white dots filled his vision. Forcing himself into action, he tried to roll over to get up.

Dedrick's knee landed on one side of his head, pressing his cheek to the cold, hard floor. "I think we're done here, don't you?" Dedrick said coolly, backing off. He straightened, caught his breath for a second, and reached a hand down to Bolcan.

Struggling to accept defeat, Bolcan took Dedrick's hand. Aching all over, he got to his feet. "I had you. If not for that bag . . . "

Dedrick shuffled to the canvas sack and squatted. "Aww, look." He groaned. "We probably broke some of them." A partially unwrapped gift lay at his feet. He rifled through the bag, mumbling something.

Bolcan wanted to say something sarcastic, wanted to

harbor a grudge, but he had asked Dedrick for this opportunity. And Dedrick had granted it.

With a few breaths, Bolcan let his embarrassment and resentment fizzle out. "What are we delivering, anyway?" he asked. "And why? I don't understand the importance of Operation Gift Drop." Leaning against the wall, Bolcan wiped grit from the side of his clammy face and felt a trickle of wetness on his forehead. It stung as he wiped it. A glance at his finger showed a dark smear that he assumed was blood in the dim light.

Holding his side and grimacing, Dedrick straightened and handed Bolcan the half-wrapped gift. "Check it out. And figure a way to wrap that thing back up. It must've had a tie." His gaze dropped to the ground.

Curious about the gift, Bolcan pulled the fabric wrapping back. A decorative wooden box held a tiny carved owl and a long strip of thick paper with something Aldonians rarely saw—handwritten words. "What is this?"

Easing his jacket on and wincing, Dedrick looked up. "Oh, that's a bookmark." He took it from Bolcan and flipped it over. "They usually write an invitation to faith on one side and a Christmas verse on the other. A verse, uh, from the Bible. Do you know what I'm talking about?"

"Of course." Bolcan acted like the question offended him, but it was a reasonable one. Aldonians were raised without faith, without sacraments, without church, and without Bibles. He'd heard about it all from various members of the Mosheh, though, both colonist and

Aldonian believers. They'd likely read from the Bible at that Mass he'd attended too.

Dedrick picked up the red hats and the flashlight, which he then shined along the ground around them.

Tilting the bookmark to the light, Bolcan read the verse to himself, the meaning at first eluding him, then a strange sensation prickling his skin and touching him in some deep place. He stuffed the bookmark back into the box and arranged the soft wrapping over it.

"Oh, here." Grunting as he stooped, Dedrick snatched something off the ground. "It was probably tied with this." He came up to Bolcan with a length of twine and tied the gift while Bolcan held it.

"A bookmark seems like a useless gift. Aldonians only read electronic books or listen to audio. Physical books belong in museums." Bolcan stuffed the gift back into the canvas bag and hoisted the bag off the floor.

"Yeah, I know. And the bookmarks get confiscated by the authorities—because of the verse—but the colonists still include them." Dedrick clipped his flashlight to his belt. Red marks on his cheek and chin disappeared once the light no longer shined on his face. "Maybe the verse or the invitation to faith will stick with a few people."

Bolcan lifted the bag higher, ready to swing it over his shoulder.

"Oh, hey, I'll take that." After adjusting the red hat on his head, Dedrick took the bag from Bolcan and swung it over his shoulder, the action making him wince.

It took Bolcan a moment to respond. "But you won."

The humble tilt of Dedrick's head contrasted with his crooked grin. "I wouldn't have. If not for you tripping on the bag. You really had me there." He turned and started off down the tunnel.

Stunned, Bolcan didn't move for a second but then bolted after him, one knee screaming as he hurried to catch up. "You're admitting I would've won?"

Dedrick shrugged. "Yeah, I admit it. And, hey, sorry about the crack against Aldonians. But you really get under my skin sometimes."

"*I* get under *your* skin?"

Bolcan donned his droopy red hat, and the two of them walked side by side at a less aggressive pace than earlier.

"So now you know what we're delivering." Dedrick readjusted the canvas bag he carried over his shoulder. "Homemade gifts. Things like yo-yos, stuffed toys, candy, soaps, little stuff that the colonists make all year long. And the reason we do it is we're celebrating Christmas."

"I figured as much. We learned about Christmas in school. It was a commercial holiday invented by capitalists so that people would spend more money."

Dedrick laughed. "No, Bolcan, Christmas is a celebration of the gift of God the Father. Over two thousand years ago, He gave us His Son, sent Him into the world to save us. His Son, who is also God, took on human form and was born in a stable. He gave us Himself. Gave us everything. That's why we give gifts tonight."

"So we give gifts to people who have no clue what it means."

Dedrick shrugged. "Few people knew what it meant on that first Christmas night either."

They walked to the sounds of their clothing swishing, soft footfalls, and an occasional clank and drip in the distance. The steady movement worked the aches out as they plodded down one dark tunnel and another. Utility pipes lined the walls of the third tunnel they turned down. The walls came closer together, the ceiling lower.

"It's not that I think you can't fight," Dedrick said out of the blue, rubbing his side under his jacket. "Before we rescued you, I saw you take down several kids at once. And, man, you've got some power behind your punches." He glanced with a look of admiration that faded quickly. "Being one of the Mosheh, it isn't just about defending people, rescuing people from Aldonia. The Mosheh practice self-discipline. We aim for humility." He paused and adjusted the heavy bag on his shoulder, carrying it now with two hands. "Sorry I'm not the best example."

"No, you're not," Bolcan said, satisfied to hear Dedrick admit it.

Dedrick threw him a look, but he spoke without his usual hint of annoyance. "The Mosheh, we come to serve Aldonians, even though Aldonians don't know it and wouldn't welcome it."

"Aldonians are raised to bow to a controlling government, to serve and obey without having the freedom to think and choose." It burned Bolcan to know that Dedrick, who hadn't experienced such a life, would probably never understand. "The Mosheh rescue people from oppression so they no longer have to live like slaves. Whether a member has humility or not, the Mosheh are not—and have never been—slaves."

"Freedom without humility is another form of slavery," Dedrick said, his tone critical. "To be Mosheh is to serve."

"I want to save, not to serve." Bolcan's jaw tensed. "I have the skills I need to do that. I have self-discipline."

Dedrick looked at him and huffed. "You were trying to use the sleeper hold on me. Were you seriously planning to knock me out?"

Bolcan didn't answer. He hadn't thought that far ahead. If Dedrick hadn't broken away and if he couldn't have shaken off his fighting instinct, maybe he would've. But he didn't want to remain a student in Mosheh training forever—and rendering a trainer unconscious might not work in his favor—so maybe he wouldn't have. In a real-life situation, he certainly would have knocked his opponent out.

A few minutes later, the tunnel narrowed even more so that they had to walk single-file. Pipes around them creaked and hummed and tinged.

"Almost there." Dedrick released one hand from the bag and unzipped a pocket inside his jacket. "We must work with absolute silence, and quickly. One gift on each bed, the rest on the first table we see, and we leave."

"At least one nanny is supposed to be awake at all hours."

"Right. Was it ever like that when you were growing up?" Dedrick pulled something made of fabric from his jacket pocket.

"You have a point." When Bolcan lived in Primary, many a night he'd awoken and wandered in search of a nanny only to take care of his business on his own: a glass of water, a trip to the bathroom, finding a friend to sleep with to keep the nightmares at bay.

"If we do come across one, let me handle it." Dedrick gave Bolcan a hard look that said he expected full compliance with that command.

"And how will you handle it?" He assumed Dedrick had a trick up his sleeve or a device on his TekBand.

"Don't worry about that." Dedrick unfolded and shook out the fabric, which turned out to be a second bag, this one made of thin material. Then he lowered the canvas sack to the floor and began dividing the goods.

"You had that all along?" Bolcan stared, dumbfounded. "We could've shared the load."

Dedrick flashed a smile as he transferred one last gift to the second bag and stood. "Nah, loser carries the bag, we decided, right?" He turned his attention to a panel in the wall and produced a ratchet from a pants pocket.

After breaking in through an access panel in the utility room, they eased another door open to a tidy kitchen with a single nightlight illuminating a couple of old appliances on a counter. Catching no signs of a nanny, Bolcan followed Dedrick down a hallway that ended at a large dark bedroom. A hint of antiseptic and ammonia carried on the sleepy air. A tiny green light over the bathroom gave form to the bunkbeds nearest it. And a tiny red dot over the nannies' bedroom illuminated a few posts of other bunkbeds, but darkness swallowed up the other rows of beds. A murmur came from one part of the room and raspy breathing from another.

A dull light appeared in Dedrick's hands. He gave the nightlight to Bolcan and pointed to the first aisle between beds. Then he pulled a gift from his bag and turned the opposite way, moving in the direction of the red and green lights.

After clipping the little light to his belt, Bolcan pulled a gift from his own canvas bag and stepped toward the first bed. Head of the bed? Foot of the bed? Remembering Dedrick's command to work quickly, he placed the gift at the foot of the top bed, placed another on the lower bed, and zipped to the next bunk while reaching for two more gifts. Moving from bunk to bunk, the rubber soles of his shoes silent, his heart racing for fear of getting caught, he unloaded the canvas bag.

What if a nanny came out? What if a child awoke? Seeing a strange man in the dark, a kid might even scream. Bolcan's heart beat harder. The nannies would rush into the room and they'd be caught. They'd be caught! He'd be caught. An image of Re-Ed flashed in his mind. Pushing it away, he focused on grabbing two more gifts and moving to the next bed.

As he turned the corner, he glimpsed Dedrick working on the last row. He wanted to finish before Dedrick did. But as his bag grew lighter, he had to reach deeper to retrieve the gifts.

Twisting toward the next bed and fumbling to grab a gift, the soft beam of his nightlight fell on the figure on the lower bunk, a seven- or eight-year-old boy who was sleeping with one arm over his head, the other straight out, and his blankets tangled around his legs.

Sadness teased Bolcan's heart. This boy should live free. They should all be free. The shoulder-length mane of pale locks and the boy's sprawled body reminded Bolcan of himself at that age. The way he thrashed around at night, he often lost his blankets by morning and awoke chilled to the bone.

Bolcan pulled the blankets up to the boy's chest and set the gift between the pillow and the headboard. Maybe the gift would still be on the bed in the morning.

A glimpse of Dedrick racing toward him snapped him from his thoughts.

"How many do you have left?" Dedrick whispered.

Bolcan reached into the bag and counted. "Eight."

"Good. I got these." Dedrick motioned to indicate the last row of bunks. "Set them on the dining room table and return to the utility room."

Anxious to get the job done now, Bolcan practically jogged down the hall, attentive to the sound of his rubber soles on the tile floor and to the mad thumping of his heart, aware that they could be caught at any second. He passed the kitchen and turned the corner too quickly.

Eyes snapping open wide, heart ready to explode, one shoe squeaking, he came to a full stop.

Someone else stood in the room. A young woman in a

long sleep shirt and loose pants had come through a dimly-lit doorway on the opposite wall. One of the nannies. She jerked back, her mouth falling open, light from a nearby nightlight revealing fear in her eyes. Then her gaze lifted to Bolcan's silly red hat.

A long table stood between them. She could easily turn back the way she had come. He could not allow her to do that. She'd call for help.

Grasping the bag to keep it from slipping from his hand, he rushed toward her. He could not allow her to scream and draw attention. He had to stop her. He could not get caught. Could not return to Re-Ed.

She stood frozen in place, staring at him through wide eyes.

As Bolcan moved around the table, his thoughts returned to the sleeper hold he'd tried to use on Dedrick. "Don't make a sound," he whispered, conveying a threat with his tone and eyes. Could he grab her around the neck and cover her mouth at the same time?

Her head shook and her mouth moved, but no words came out at first. "Who . . . are you?" she finally said, wrapping her arms around her waist. "Why are you here?"

A breath away from lunging at her, Dedrick's words shouted in his head. *We come to serve Aldonians.* The verse on the bookmark followed.

Though Jesus was in the form of God, He did not count equality with God something to be grasped at; rather He emptied Himself, taking the form of a slave, being born in the likeness of mer.

A wave of something unearthly washed over him at those words. Profound truth zipped through his mind. God who made heaven and earth, the All Powerful, who could do all things, humbled Himself, abased Himself, emptied Himself, becoming like one of His creatures. Taking the form of a slave . . . of a baby . . . of a tiny, circle-shaped bread.

God did that.

Who was Bolcan to behave with such pride? Maybe he wanted to join the Mosheh for all the wrong reasons. He did not see himself as a servant. Whenever he trained—especially with Dedrick—he wanted to prove that he was not just capable, but better. He couldn't even go on this little mission without challenging Dedrick to a fight. He knew everything. He could do everything. On his own. Dedrick had tried to explain it to him: humility was needed to be Mosheh, humility that imitated their God. To save, He served.

Bolcan stopped an arm's-length away from the nanny and fell to one knee. "I-I come as a servant. Don't be afraid."

She shook her head again, confusion in her eyes. "A servant? What?"

He pushed a damp lock of hair from his forehead and considered how to explain. "I'm sure you've heard others speak of receiving gifts on one special night."

"Oh . . . yes, I-I thought that was just made up. A silly rumor."

Despite the slight trembling in his body, Bolcan pushed his fear back and smiled, wanting to gain her trust. He could do this. "It's real. This is the night and that's why I'm here." He stuffed his hand in the bag and withdrew a gift. "See? This is for you. But it's my mission to deliver these without being caught." Peering up at her, he gave her a flirtatious grin. "Looks like I blew that."

Fear left her expression, she released her tense hold on her abdomen, swung her hands to her sides and smiled. "Oh, wow," she whispered, sounding awestruck. "Thank you." Then she bounced on her toes and pointed over her shoulder. "I'm going back to bed." She gave him one last smile, the pink in her cheeks visible even with the scant light, and she dashed from the room.

Bolcan exhaled and doubled over, slapping his palms to the floor as the trembling seized him. He didn't move for a moment, not sure what had just happened to him.

A swishing sound came from behind, then Dedrick's whispered voice. "Bolcan, you okay?" He grabbed Bolcan's arm and tugged, helping him up.

Bolcan looked at the bag with the remaining gifts and froze.

Dedrick whipped the last gifts out and set them on the table. "We gotta go." Clutching the empty bag with one hand, he wrapped an arm around Bolcan's shoulders and forced him to move.

Some time later, Bolcan sat leaning against the cold wall of a dark tunnel, Dedrick at his side, the details of how he got there a bit blurry. His heart had calmed completely, and his sweaty neck gave him a chill. What had happened to him? Must've been one of his panic attacks.

He didn't want to see the look in Dedrick's eyes. Though he still had nightmares, he hadn't had an attack like this in months. Maybe even over a year. Would it disqualify him from performing rescue missions?

Dedrick's head turned, no look of condemnation in his eyes. "Well?" Sitting with his legs stretched out before him, he took a deep breath and rubbed his thighs. "We ready to get going?"

Bolcan climbed to his feet, his strength and mind restored.

Dedrick handed him the empty canvas sack. "You can carry this one. I've got the other." He tapped his jacket pocket and grinned.

They walked side by side through one dark tunnel and another to the pick-up point, Bolcan ready for the lecture that never came. Dedrick talked on and on about his family Christmas traditions back home—wherever that was. They decorated pine trees, baked special cookies, attended Midnight Mass, and exchanged gifts in the morning. He said nothing about Bolcan's panic attack or the success or failure of the mission. Did it matter that the nanny had seen him? Dedrick likely realized it. Maybe he'd even seen Bolcan on his knee before her. What would Dedrick have done in that situation?

The tunnel kart came into view, and the cheerful voices of the other young Mosheh members telling tales of the night carried through the cold, dark tunnels. Compelled to know the answer, Bolcan whacked Dedrick's arm to stop him.

Dedrick checked his TekBand then gave Bolcan his full attention.

He struggled for a second with whether he should bring it up at all, but then the words tumbled out. "Do you know a nanny caught me?"

"Yeah." Dedrick looked unfazed.

"You told me to let you handle it but . . . well, you were in the other room."

"No, actually, I was a few seconds behind you."

"Oh." Bolcan averted his gaze, embarrassed at the thought of Dedrick seeing the whole thing, but then curious. "Why didn't you intervene? My first impulse was to use a sleeper hold. On the girl."

A smile flickered on Dedrick's face then faded. "That would not have been a good idea."

"How would you have handled it?"

The smile returned. "I like what you did. It was very humble." He cupped Bolcan's shoulder and proceeded toward the tunnel kart.

Early the next morning at the Mosheh Control Center, having caught only a few restless hours of sleep after the night's adventure, Bolcan stood with other young Mosheh members, watching an array of surveillance videos, the live feed coming from the government's intrusive Citizen Safety Station.

Children in primary and secondary facilities sat on each other's beds and in groups in the bedrooms, appreciating their gifts. The nannies, who normally clung to the schedule, let the children have their fun while they marveled at their own little gifts. Bolcan spotted the nanny from last night. Her smile was bigger than the others, but then, she alone had seen one of the mysterious deliverers of these gifts.

The rest of the Mosheh reported no incident. They'd crept into factories, grocery stores, government buildings, and the hospital, delivering gifts undetected. A few brave souls had even delivered gifts to the Citizen Safety Station for the workers who supposedly watched Aldonia day and night.

As Bolcan gazed at the monitors, the verse on the bookmark played in his mind, comforting him, challenging him, striking him somewhere so deep that he knew he would never be the same. "Though He was in the form of God, He did not count equality with God something to be grasped at; rather He emptied Himself, taking the form of a slave, being born in the likeness of men."

He could not comprehend such a humble act from the Almighty One. And he had to admit that Dedrick had something of that humility too, despite his over cautiousness and inflexibility with rules. Now Bolcan hungered for more of the traditions and gifts and the faith that the colonists had, the faith that allowed them to be both free and servant at the same time.

In imitation of their God.

*****

If you'd like to know more about Dedrick, Bolcan, the underground Mosheh, and the dystopian world these characters live in, check out the Chasing Liberty trilogy. You'll meet Liberty, a young Aldonian woman who desperately wants to avoid her government-assigned vocation. She has two weeks to escape but little hope of success until she encounters the secret group you met in this short story. You can also read "Bound to Find Freedom," another short story prequel to the trilogy. It is available for free at www.CatholicTeenBooks.com.

ABOUT THE AUTHOR

THERESA LINDEN is the author of the *Chasing Liberty* dystopian trilogy and the *West Brothers* series, including Catholic Press Association award-winners *Roland West, Loner* and *Battle for His Soul*. She resides in Ohio with her husband and their three teen sons. A Secular Franciscan and a member of the Catholic Writers Guild, her faith inspires the belief that there is no greater adventure than the realities we can't see, the spiritual side of life. She hopes that her stories will spark her readers' imaginations and awaken them to the power of faith and grace. Learn more about her and find her social media links at www.TheresaLinden.com.

CHRISTMAS ANGEL

by Leslea Wahl

The sanctuary sparkles brilliantly. Twinkling purple lights peek from boughs of greenery adorning the church in a joyous atmosphere. A single tall Advent candle flickers, casting a warm glow on the wooden crèche next to it.

The first Sunday of Advent means we have arrived at my favorite time of year. The Christmas season is upon us. At last. I'm giddy with expectation as I try to focus on the celebration of the Mass.

For weeks now, I've looked forward to hearing festive carols fill the airways and watching sappy, romantic holiday movies. The youth group will hold its secret Santa party, and my family will take its annual outing to see *The Nutcracker* performed. Mom and I will soon spend hours baking and decorating dozens of scrumptious sugar cookies. My mouth waters just thinking about the frosted treats.

Ah, truly the most wonderful time of year.

"I want to leave you with one final thought." Father Brady's baritone voice shatters my Sugar Plum Fairy reverie.

I straighten in my pew. Had I missed everything he's said? *Come on, Meg, focus.*

His slow scan of the congregation fills the priest's dramatic pause. His roaming gaze seems to stop when he focuses on mine. "I encourage you all to pray and ask for God's guidance in how you can personally make this Advent more meaningful. Make this the year you truly keep Christ in Christmas."

With that brief but—at least to me—powerful line, he was finished.

Keep Christ in Christmas. I mentally kick myself for having daydreamed through the rest of his message. Well, at least I'd caught the recap.

I force myself to stay tuned in during the rest of Mass. As we exit the church, I turn to Mom. "The church was so pretty. It really put me in the Christmas spirit. When can we finish decorating?"

She shoots me a smile. "How about tomorrow after school?"

I shake my head. "No can do. I promised Rachael I'd go shopping with her. If that's okay."

She links her arm through mine. "Only if you promise to buy me something spectacular."

I feign shock. "Don't I always?" I remember the numerous handmade creations I used to give her every year. "Let me rephrase. Haven't I given you something amazing the last few years?"

She smiles and leans her head on my shoulder. "You do

a wonderful job of finding meaningful gifts, but I do miss the days when you hand-crafted my gifts with those precious little fingers. They'll always be some of my most treasured possessions."

I roll my eyes…but I know she means every word. Each year, she still brings out the horrendous decorations I crafted. The paper reindeer with antlers made from my traced handprints. The misshapen clay snowman that looks more like something the cat might have coughed up than a Christmas heirloom. The toilet paper rolls with glued-on scraps of material that were supposed to resemble a nativity scene—an especially embarrassing treasure.

I sigh, but I'm not really bothered by Mom's sentimentality. Reminiscing about all the decorations from Christmases past is another tradition of the season.

As Rachael and I stroll through the mall, my senses absorb the holiday atmosphere. Huge, shiny ornaments dangle from the towering two-story ceiling. Familiar, beloved tunes of reindeer and silver bells fill the air, and the scent of cinnamon makes me smile. It's beginning to look a lot like Christmas, indeed. Yet my contentment is shadowed somewhat. As I watch the growing line of kids waiting to see Santa, Father Brady's words at Mass pop into my mind. *Keep Christ in Christmas.* I never really thought about it before, but as festive as the mall feels, there is nothing that reflects the true meaning of Christmas. There is not a Nativity scene in sight.

"Hello. Earth to Meg."

I glance at Rachael. "Oh. Sorry. What were you saying?"

"I was asking if you think I should ask Jackson to the sleigh ride."

"Oh, sure. Good idea." My friend's crush *du jour* is the furthest thing from my mind.

Her eyebrows furrow. "You okay?"

I nod. "Yeah. Just distracted."

"Okay. Hey, look." She points to one of our favorite stores. "All their sweaters are on sale. I've been shopping for other people all afternoon. Maybe it's time for a little something for myself."

I glance one last time at the line of excited kids, their tired-looking parents, and the pointy-shoed elf handing out candy canes before I'm yanked into the store.

She heads straight for a table of fuzzy sweaters. I follow along and run my hand along the soft material as she sorts through them.

"Why are you so out of it today?" Rachael glances my way as she begins choosing sweaters.

"My priest said something at Mass on Sunday that keeps ringing through my head." I don't share the fact that it was really the only thing that I heard him say. "He said to remember to keep Christ in Christmas."

She shoves the pile of sweaters into my arms, then turns to a rack of shirts. "That's a cool saying."

"Yeah, but I think Father Brady meant it as more than a saying."

"What do you mean?" She scans a flowery blouse then

flicks the hanger aside to check out the next selection.

"Well, what was he suggesting? How does a person keep Christ in Christmas?"

She shrugs as she continues to flip through the clothes. "Your family has a Nativity scene out on your lawn, and your mom always sends out religious Christmas cards. I'd say your family does its part."

I shift the pile of sweaters from one arm to the other and lean against the sweater table. "I don't know." I think back to the way Father's gaze seemed to lock on mine. "Maybe he means we should act more like Jesus? You know, sacrifice ourselves for others. Do things we wouldn't normally do to keep our focus on Christ."

Rachael grabs another blouse, along with the pile of sweaters in my arms, and then strides toward the fitting room. "I'll be right back," she calls over her shoulder.

I walk around the racks of clothes, lost in thought. How do you keep Christ in Christmas? What does that mean? Then I remember Father Brady's suggestion of praying.

Okay, God, I would like to make this Christmas more meaningful. Can you help me figure out a way to do that? Give me a hint? Please?

The ear-piercing screams of a child interrupt my prayer. My head snaps up and toward the commotion. A young mother in line at the counter tries to console her near-hysterical daughter. The little girl strains against the confines of her stroller, her tear-stained cheeks bright red.

"Amelia, we'll leave in a few minutes. Mommy just needs to pay, then we'll head home for your nap."

The little girl answers with another shriek. A slightly older woman ahead of them in line shoots the young mother a disgusted look.

The frenzied mom squats next to the stroller. That's when I notice—amid the bundle of clothes in her arms, she's holding a tiny baby. The poor lady has her hands full in more ways than one. "Shh… It's okay, Amelia, you've been such a good girl. We'll leave in just a few minutes."

The exhausted toddler draws a small arm back and throws a sippy cup with all her might. Almost in unison, several shoppers gasp. The cup rolls across the tile floor and lands near my feet. In the loaded silence that follows, I glance at the cup, then at the mom. Her eyes fill with tears.

I pick up the discarded item and make my way to the line. The little girl grows quiet, her gaze wary as she watches me approach with her prized possession. I smile and she sniffles in response. As I hand the cup into the chubby little fingers, I suddenly know what I need to do. I glance around to make sure no one I know is in the store, then I lean close. "Hi, I'm Megan. Want to hear a story?"

The little one nods, even as a single tear slips down her flushed cheek. I sit on the cold floor next to her and make up a tale about a polar bear. Her gaze fixes on me as the tale takes shape and her mom inches closer to the front of the line. I demonstrate the polar bear's expressions, and the little girl giggles. Her sweet smile strengthens my confidence and the polar bear's antics grow even more elaborate.

Before long the young mother is finished checking out.

She places her bag in the back of the stroller. I quickly finish the polar bear's adventure and tell my little friend goodbye. When I'm on my feet again, Amelia's mom wraps me in a long, tight hug.

"You are a Christmas angel," she whispers in my ear. "Thank you so much."

As she pushes Amelia out of the store, I suddenly have my answer about how I can keep Christ in Christmas this Advent. I will sacrifice of myself and do a good deed every day until December 25th.

"Meg, you're not being very helpful," Rachael whines.

We're in line at the local coffee shop a week later. I roll my eyes. Sometimes my friend's focus on herself is a little wearing.

"There's only a few days left until the sleigh ride," she persists. "Should I ask Jackson to go with me or not?"

"I already told you I think you should." My mouth waters as I eye the gooey cinnamon roll in the display case. I've been craving one all day.

I grow hungrier by the moment in the slow-moving line. We're sandwiched between an elderly gentleman behind us, whose black baseball cap indicates he's a veteran, and a guy at the front of the line with messy hair that probably took much longer to style than mine.

"But do you think he likes me?" Rachael asks. "I mean, it would be weird to ask him to go if he just thinks of me as a friend."

"Just invite him to go with a group of us, then it won't

be weird, and you'll get to know him better." Mr. Trying-Too-Hard-Not-To-Look-Cool still has not budged. He's too busy flirting with the cute cashier rocking a Santa hat to notice the long line behind him.

Rachael nods. "Yeah, that sounds good. Then there's no pressure."

Finally, the coffee-shop Romeo moves out of the way. The cashier shoots him one last, dazzling smile, the end of her Santa hat swaying with the turn of her head. "What can I get started for you ladies?"

After Rachael recites her complicated order, I ask for one of their seasonal specials, the Merry Mocha, and a cinnamon roll. The cashier rings up the order, and I reach into my purse for my wallet. Out of the corner of my eye I see the scuffed shoes of the man standing behind us. I glance up over my shoulder at him. His wrinkled face crinkles even more with a crooked grin. I return the smile and turn back to the cashier.

With a final, longing look at the delectable treat in the display case, I place the money in her outstretched hand. "Um, actually can you forget the cinnamon roll and instead use the extra money to pay for the order of the gentleman behind us?"

The woman stares at me like I'd just asked her to stand on the counter and sing a Christmas song at the top of her lungs. "Excuse me?"

I smile. "I'd like to pay for his order."

The confused worker's gaze drops to the money I'm offering. "Really?"

"Really?" Rachael echoes, equally astonished.

"Really," I answer then walk toward a high-top table near the front window.

Rachael sits across from me. "What was that about?"

I shrug. "It's just something I'm trying this Advent, helping others."

"Is this about that whole keeping Christ in Christmas thing?" She hangs her jacket on the back of her chair.

I watch as the cashier points our way and the older gentleman sends me a smile that warms my insides faster than a Merry Mocha. "Yeah. I took Father Brady's advice and prayed for a way to make Advent more meaningful. I'm sure it's different for everyone. Maybe for some people it would be going to daily Mass or doing an Advent study or something. But this is the idea that came to me, doing little things for strangers."

Rachael tips her head to me. "Well, I know what a sacrifice it was for you to give up that decadent pastry. So, good job."

We watch as the sweet gentleman shuffles our way carrying three beverages in festive cups. He sets two down on our table. His watery eyes and crooked smile make me want to wrap my arms around him. However, I resist the temptation to hug a total stranger.

"I asked the barista if I could deliver your drinks so I could thank you for buying my coffee this morning. What a wonderful start to my day."

"You are very welcome. Merry Christmas—and thank you for your service."

He tips his hat, then exits the coffee shop.

Rachael reaches for her drink. "So, you've been doing good deeds for over a week now and I didn't even notice? Why didn't you tell me?"

I laugh. "I'm not doing it for the recognition. I just want to help." While we enjoy our drinks, I tell her what I've been up to. Shoveling snow for my neighbor on that ridiculously cold day, missing part of lunch break to help my history teacher rearrange his classroom, giving up my seat on the bus, helping an elderly woman carry her groceries to her car.

"Wow. That's really cool. So, is it making Christmas more special?"

I freeze as I ponder her question, my coffee in midair. While I feel good about helping people, I can't decide if I'm really doing anything worthwhile. Can any of it be defined as keeping Christ in Christmas? I mean, Jesus really made a difference. He wasn't just nice to folks—He changed their lives. Am I missing something? "Um . . . yeah. Even though they're small gestures, I'm serving others, which amazingly makes me focus more on Jesus and not just myself. I don't know if it's really making any difference to the people I help, though."

Rachael sets her coffee on the table. "Why wouldn't it? Even small gestures can make a difference. You're letting people know that someone notices and cares about them. That's pretty amazing."

Her words remind me of a song we used to sing in Sunday school, "They Will Know We Are Christians By

Our Love." Helping others was the idea that came to me after I prayed. My kind yet simple, loving gestures will have to be enough.

Rachael's eyes light up. "You know, it's such a great idea. Maybe I'll try it as well."

The days leading up to Christmas pass in a flurry of activity. Between the holiday fun of sledding, caroling, shopping, and the million other fun things that fill the season, I make sure to carve out time each day to do a good deed for someone—a hodge-podge of small actions to help others.

Sometimes I wasn't sure who to help, but then I'd feel a little nudge toward a particular person. A few times I tried to negotiate with God, like when the task I felt called to help with didn't really fit into my schedule. Like spending my whole Saturday baking, decorating, and delivering cookies to the firehouse. Or missing an afternoon at the movies with my friends to help a fellow church member, a woman who'd broken her arm, wrap her Christmas gifts. But when those moments hit, I remembered all that Jesus had done for me. I mean, it was hard to complain about being a little inconvenienced when I thought about how He died on the cross for me. I even began to tell people why I was helping, to keep Christ in Christmas. Amazingly, no one looked at me like I had three heads. Everyone said it was a wonderful idea and thanked me over and over again.

Christmas Eve has finally arrived.

I'm seated at a café table waiting for Rachael. In just a few hours, my family will enjoy dinner and game night before attending Midnight Mass with my grandparents, our usual tradition. But no matter how much I look forward to the fun, I can't shake my distracted frustration.

I kept thinking my last good deed would be something unique and meaningful to mark the end of my Advent adventure. My own beautiful gift to give Jesus on His birthday. But the Holy Spirit must already be celebrating the birth of Christ because I haven't received any inspiring internal prompts. Time is running out.

Rachael enters the room, quickly scans it, and spots me. She waves and makes her way through the crowded café. "Thanks for meeting me for lunch, Meg. I wanted to give you your present before Christmas."

She hands me a festive bag, and I give her the wrapped box I brought for her. We open the gifts and spend a few minutes *oohing* and *aahing* at what's inside. I immediately wrap my new oh-so-soft scarf around my neck. Rachael's present is one of the other sweaters she'd liked when she was able to buy only one.

"Oh!" Her eyes widen in excitement. "I almost forgot to tell you! Jackson and I have been texting back and forth all week."

"That's great." Judging by the starry look in her eyes, I'm not sure she even hears me.

"I mean, I still don't know if he likes me, but it's fun getting to know him." She lets out a dramatic sigh. "Just

think, when near-disaster happened, and I stepped on his hand climbing into the sleigh that night, I thought for sure all hope was lost! I mean, why would he like someone who nearly ruined his basketball career? But now it's kind of become an inside joke."

I only answer with a grin.

She rolls her eyes then fills me in on her Christmas week plans to go skiing with her family.

After the waitress comes and we order our soups and salads, Rachael turns her attention to me. "So, have you finished your campaign to keep Christ in Christmas?"

My shoulders sag. "No. I really thought my final act would be something impactful. You know, some incredible grand finale. I've been praying about it, but the right idea just hasn't come to me."

She shakes her head. "You don't need a grand finale. This whole idea of yours has made a bigger difference than you realize. My random acts of kindness were all met with such gratitude that a few people decided to do their own good deeds. Without knowing it, you reached a lot of people."

"Really? That's amazing." Maybe that was the whole point of this process—to encourage people to forget themselves and care for others this season. Every time I helped someone, especially when it involved something I didn't feel like doing, I thought about God and how much He has done for me. By doing special things for others, I was drawn closer to Christ. What if, in some small way, my deeds had a ripple effect and brought others closer to

Christ as well? That would be incredible.

My heart patters. I can't wait to tell Father Brady how his simple words made such an impact.

Rachael reaches for her water. "Well, now that Christmas has arrived, you can go back to your normal life."

I stare at her and realize that part of my unsettled feeling is a sadness that my good-deeds campaign is over. That grand finale I was expecting would surely make it all feel complete.

As the waitress delivers our food, the first thought bombards my mind—loud and clear, like silver bells and angelic trumpets in one big blast.

Pay for that woman's meal.

I actually look around to see who voiced the command.

"What's wrong?" Rachael glances around as well.

"Um… Nothing. I thought I heard something."

I shake my head, reach for my fork—and it happens again.

Pay for the woman's meal.

Rachael dips a chunk of bread into her soup without a care in the world.

I slowly look around. Everyone else in the restaurant is eating, chatting, or laughing. They are all completely unaware of the commanding voice. *Am I the only one who heard that? Whoa.* A shiver runs down my spine.

What was that? Could it be…*God?* But this is so different than the gentle nudges He's used to guide me all Advent.

I slowly scan the crowded restaurant searching for someone in need. The last of my hard-earned babysitting money sits in my bank account. Maybe someone needs it more than I do. But as I look at my fellow diners, no one appears to need help paying for their meal. Finally, my gaze settles on a woman a few tables away. She's sitting alone, absently swirling a fork through her pasta. Her tailored suit and perfect, coiffed hair tell me it's unlikely she's in need of my help. I must be misunderstanding.

Pay for the woman's meal.

This time I know it's Him. A twinge of fear is quickly replaced by a sense of calm, and I know beyond a shadow of a doubt that I'm experiencing some kind of Divine moment. Something completely different than anything I've ever experienced.

I wanted my last deed to be something unique. Well, what could be more special than getting a calling from God on Christmas Eve? I focus my attention on the lone diner once again. French-manicured fingers slide her plate away. She dabs her mouth with her napkin then lays it on the table next to her discarded plate. All tell-tale signs that she's finished eating and the waitress will soon bring her check.

Pay for the woman's meal.

I swallow the lump in my throat. Okay. I set down my fork and motion for the waitress.

"Can I get you something?" Our friendly server responds at once.

"Umm… Yeah. See that woman over there, the one by

herself?" I discreetly point across the room.

The waitress follows my gaze. "Yes."

Rachael looks up. Soup spills off her spoon.

I ignore the surprised look on my friend's face and reach into my wallet for my debit card. "I'd like to pay for her meal."

"She a friend of yours?" the waitress asks.

I shake my head. "No. I've never met her."

The waitress's quizzical look only lasts a second then she takes my card. "Okay, sure thing."

She disappears, and Rachael sets down her now-empty spoon. "Why that woman? She doesn't exactly look needy."

My shoulders raise and lower in a shrug. "I don't know. I just know that she's the one I'm supposed to help today. I guess she's the grand finale."

My friend glances at the woman, obviously thinking the same thing I had—that this woman is an odd recipient of my final good deed. "I thought you were hoping for something special."

I sigh. "Me too, but this voice inside my head keeps telling me that she's the one."

Rachael's eyes widen. "Whoa."

The waitress brings back my card. "That's a really nice gesture. Maybe I'll have to do an act of Christmas kindness myself today. It's a great idea."

"Thanks. Please don't tell her who paid for the lunch. I'd rather keep it anonymous."

"Really?"

I nod. "I'm not doing it for any kind of recognition. I'm just trying to keep Christ in Christmas."

She tilts her head. "Sure, whatever you say."

We watch as the waitress heads over to tell the woman someone paid for her meal. Expecting a smile or a surprised look, I'm totally unprepared when the recipient of my final good deed bursts into tears.

The waitress glances at me.

Oh no. Bewildered, I shrug in response. The poor waitress obviously has no idea what to do and slowly slinks away. The elegant woman's shoulders shake as she sobs. People at nearby tables turn to watch the unexpected outburst.

I look at Rachael as panic washes through me. "I didn't mean to upset her. What do I do?"

My friend slowly shakes her head. "I have no idea."

I glance back at the woman. All I'd wanted was to make someone's day a little better. Not ruin it. Leave it to me to misread a decree from the Lord. "I guess I should go 'fess up and apologize."

With a deep breath, I gather my courage and force myself to walk across the room, ignoring the curious faces of the other customers. As I approach, the woman glances up at me. Her perfect makeup is now streaked with tears.

Afraid I'll upset her even more, I slowly slide into the seat across from her. "I'm so sorry. I'm the one who paid for your meal. I didn't mean to upset you. I've just been doing a good deed for someone every day of Advent."

Her expression is so blank that for a moment I wonder

if she understands English. Then she reaches for her napkin and dabs her eyes. "I don't understand." She clears her throat. "Why did you choose me?"

Is she upset because she thinks I assume she needs help? I glance down at my hands then back at her. "I don't really know. I just had this overwhelming feeling that I was supposed to pay for your meal."

The woman's face pales and her eyes fill with tears again. I feel like fleeing the uncomfortable situation but know I can't abandon her.

She takes a few deep breaths as she gathers her composure. "My daughter died earlier this year." She twists the napkin with trembling fingers. "I've been so devastated and didn't know how to go on. This morning I prayed for a sign that we both would be okay." Her teary eyes meet mine. "You are my answer to prayer."

My breath catches in my throat. "Me? An answer to prayer?" It never dawned on me that God might be using my acts of kindness to answer other people's prayers.

She gives me a small quivering smile. "God works in mysterious ways." She reaches out and places her beautifully manicured hand on mine. "You are truly my Christmas angel."

Now, as I return the lady's smile, I'm the one blinking back tears. Talk about a grand finale! This woman needed a sign from God, and I was the instrument He used to deliver it. Wow!

Thank you, Lord!

The most incredible feeling flows through my entire

being as the pieces of my Advent journey suddenly all fit together. God loves us so much that He sent us His precious Son as a babe in a manger on that first Christmas so long ago. Christ is the most precious gift we ever received, and He is the most precious gift that we can give. If we are willing to keep the love of Christ in our hearts and lead others to Him through these acts of love, we are indeed keeping Christ in Christmas. Just because Advent is over doesn't mean my actions need to end. By serving others through Him, I can keep Christ alive all year long.

Keep Christ in Christmas. This is a phrase we often hear during the holidays, but have you ever stopped to think what those words actually mean? Amid all the excitement and busyness of the season, how could you make Christmas even more meaningful? Leslea Wahl's "Christmas Angel" explores this idea. As you follow Meg's journey of discovering what these words mean for her life, maybe you will also discover a special way to keep Christ in your Christmas this year.

ABOUT THE AUTHOR

LESLEA WAHL is the author of the award-winning Catholic teen mysteries *The Perfect Blindside, An Unexpected Role, Where You Lead,* and *eXtreme Blindside.* Her journey to become an author came through a search for value-based fiction for her own children. She now not only writes for teens but also has become a reviewer of Catholic teen fiction to help other families find faith-based books. Leslea lives in beautiful Colorado with her husband and children. The furry, four-legged members of her family often make cameo appearances in her novels. Leslea has always loved mysteries and hopes to encourage teens to grow in their faith through these fun adventures. For more information about her faith-filled Young Adult mysteries please visit www.LesleaWahl.com.

SIGNS OF CHRISTMAS

by Cynthia T. Toney

One at a time, Antonina placed her new T-strap patent-leather pumps in the bottom of the chifforobe, careful to leave space between them. She pointed the toes toward the back so she could admire the curved Louis heels—all the rage for Christmas 1925—each time she opened the door to get her coat. The pumps were her first pair of grown-up-style shoes after turning fourteen, and she longed to show them off to her best friend.

Sal.

She sighed, closing and latching the chifforobe's door.

This would be their first Christmas apart. She had not heard from Salvatore since he and his parents left Louisiana for parts unknown over three months ago. And he had told her not to expect to hear from him, because they were escaping the wrath of organized crime. Some people called it the Mafia. But all Antonina knew was the ache in her heart from missing Sal.

Rain beating at a sharp angle against her second-story

bedroom window did nothing to improve her mood. The dreary view of the courtyard below held no sign that a glorious Christmas neared. If not for Christmas cards and a decorated tree in the living room to prove otherwise, the morning could've been any other since Sal's departure.

Why couldn't this Christmas, of all Christmases, with her sadness that even new shoes couldn't diminish, bring snow to brighten the landscape of Freedom and the farms surrounding it? At least snow would cover all signs of Sal, such as the camellia bushes they used to sit under at his place. She'd had to avert her eyes every time her family drove by Sal's old farm.

Each night and throughout each day since he left, she'd prayed for Sal's safety. And for God to give her a sign that he was all right.

She sniffed and turned away from the window. Better to put her mind to planning which dress she'd wear for Christmas Mass. None was new, but the pumps would make any of her dresses appear more sophisticated. And maybe she could beg her older sister, Dorothea, to borrow a necklace.

Antonina pulled a dark green dress by its hanger from the chifforobe. Not only was it a perfect Christmas color, but it was the best color with her red hair. She held the dress against her chest and viewed herself in the mirrors mounted on the chifforobe doors. Yes, it would work well with the shoes and her new cream-colored stockings. She hung the dress back up and plopped on the edge of her bed. If only the weather would change soon, so she

wouldn't have to slosh through puddles to reach Papa's car behind their restaurant and then again outside the church. Her new shoes wouldn't last long with that kind of treatment.

Dorothea poked her head through the doorway of their shared room. "Stop moping and come help Mama and me make the cookies." She didn't wait for Antonina's answer.

Bossy. Just because Dorothea was two and a half years older.

Antonina gathered her hair, twisting it into a bun. She pinned it behind her head and hurried to join Dorothea.

In the kitchen, Antonina slipped the bib of an apron over her head, and Mama tied the sashes behind her back. Maybe making the traditional Sicilian Christmas cookies would lift her spirits. At least it was an activity that didn't remind her of Sal.

Rolling the dough between her palms for the chocolate balls and cherry balls was always her job. Next year she'd ask to make the sesame-seed *giugiuleni*. They required more skill, and the adults who ate them criticized when they weren't perfect. This year, she didn't care to learn anything new. She would still enjoy licking sweet icing off her fingers after making the chocolate and cherry balls.

As she rolled the dough, she began to silently pray a rosary for Sal and his family. Praying they would stay safe and have a good Christmas despite their circumstances. And that someday Sal would come back, or at least let her know where he was. *Please, God, give me a sign to ease my worry.*

"Antonina, pay attention to what you're doing! The balls are all different sizes!" Dorothea scowled.

Antonina blinked hard. Dorothea was right. Her work was not up to Mama's standards.

But Mama smiled tenderly at her.

Antonina exhaled with relief. After Sal had said goodbye, Mama had comforted Antonina with a big, soft hug and soothing words as Antonina cried, lying face down on her bed. Dorothea, with her sharp words about everything, must've taken after someone else in the family.

With the final batches of chocolate and cherry balls baked, cooled, and glazed, Antonina asked to be excused. She escaped downstairs to the family's restaurant.

Antonina sat at a table close to the window, leaning her chin in her hand, and peered out. The rain had slowed, but even if it stopped, the likelihood of the Labato family restaurant filling with patrons was slim two days before Christmas Eve. Everyone in town usually kept busy cooking and baking for their arriving visitors and their own holiday meals. An occasional stranger might stop in when traveling through town.

Antonina dropped her hand and squinted.

A girl crossed the street and walked straight toward the restaurant. She wore a ragged coat and a faded skirt, and her thin legs ended in men's boots much too large for her feet. Newspaper poked out of their tops and blocked holes in the toes. She hesitated at the entrance.

No one ever dressed so poorly to eat at the restaurant. The girl must've been lost or looking for someone.

Antonina stood and opened the door. "What do you want?" Misty rain dampened her face like the girl's.

The girl shifted her weight, and a section of blonde hair fell from under her knit cap.

Antonina's eyes opened wide. "Oh, I know you. You were at my school when it started in the fall."

The girl, Lucy Morgan, had been placed two grades lower than Antonina. She looked older than that, although skinny as a rail. In September, she was the only girl not wearing shoes, but the weather was warm at the time. She didn't show up again after the first few weeks.

The girl opened her mouth to speak, but Papa appeared next to Antonina.

"Antonina, go get the brown paper bag I left in the restaurant kitchen."

She glanced at Papa's stoic face. "Yes, Papa." She hurried and returned with the heavy bag.

"Please wish your mama a Merry Christmas from us." Papa extended the package to the girl.

With a tiny smile, Lucy nodded and accepted his gift. "Thank you, sir."

When the door again separated the girl from them, Papa patted Antonina's shoulder. "Just some sweet potatoes and vegetables. Her papa passed away in October." He cleared his throat and returned to his kitchen.

Antonina swallowed hard. Poor Lucy. No wonder she didn't have decent shoes or clothing. How fortunate for the Labato family to own a business that could help them survive hard times. Even if Papa passed away—and Antonina hated to think about it—she and her mother and sister could run the restaurant and continue to make a living.

Antonina's gaze fell to her boots. She lifted her head and trotted upstairs.

Antonina stood in the dining room doorway as Mama arranged poinsettias and Christmas decorations in the center of the gleaming mahogany table.

Without looking up, Mama said, "Whatever's on your mind, make yourself useful while you think. Take one of these dust rags and clean under the table."

Antonina took a rag and crawled to the nearest of two supporting pedestals that separated into three legs with ball-and-claw feet. As she ran her rag over the wood, she said, "What are we going to do with all those cookies?"

"Same thing we do every year. Serve them to our restaurant guests and share them with our neighbors and family that visit us."

"May I have a few for a friend?" Antonina crawled out from under the table.

Mama turned to face her. "Of course." Her brow furrowed.

Maybe Mama had the same thought as Antonina, that they would no longer need the cookies they usually gifted to Sal's family at Christmas.

"Thank you, Mama." Antonina finished the other

pedestal and took the dirty rag with her to the upstairs kitchen.

Antonina laid the rag on the floor next to the mop bucket and washed her hands at the deep porcelain sink. A collection of baskets sat on a shelf above her head. She drew up a chair and stood on its seat to have a look.

One small basket browned with age lay within a nest of larger baskets. *Perfect.* She took it down with her and searched for a clean cloth to wrap some cookies in.

Dorothea breezed into the kitchen carrying a sack and stopped to drink a glass of water.

"Where are you going?" Antonina spoke in her most nonchalant voice, without looking her sister in the eye.

"To take gifts to my friends, if that's any of your business."

Antonina faced Dorothea but clamped her lips shut. Although she was tempted to blurt out an equally unkind reply, she allowed Dorothea's ugly words to hang in the air without a response. Turning the other cheek had never been one of Antonina's strengths—especially where her sister was concerned—but since Antonina's last Confession, she'd made an effort to curb her anger.

Besides, Antonina really needed her sister's help.

Dorothea shrugged her shoulders and rolled her eyes. "Sorry."

Antonina held up her basket. "I have a gift to take to someone too. May I ride with you?"

"Sure." Dorothea smiled.

Even Dorothea couldn't stay mean at Christmas. Antonina smiled back.

One look at the number of children playing on the porch at Lucy's house, and Antonina figured she should've brought a hundred cookies instead of a dozen.

"I won't be but a minute." She slipped out of the car, leaving Dorothea behind the steering wheel with the motor running.

Lucy herself answered Antonina's knock at the front door. With surprise in her eyes, she said, "Hello."

Antonina smiled. "Hello." She bounced her shoulders. "May I come in?"

"Sure. Pardon my manners." Lucy wiped her hands on a dirty apron worn over men's overalls.

Antonina tore her gaze from the odd combination of clothing and offered Lucy the basket. "I thought you might like some cookies. I helped make them."

Lucy's face brightened, and she accepted the gift. "Thank you. That's so kind. The children will love them. Mama's been sick, so I do all the cooking and baking."

The children. As if she wasn't allowed to be a child herself. Unsure what to say next, Antonina glanced about inside the untidy home and then looked down at the floor.

Lucy wore battered slippers in worse condition than the boots she'd previously worn, if that were possible.

Antonina's heart rattled. Lucy's life differed so from her own.

Antonina had to get out of there. She raised her head,

took a deep breath, and released it. "Well, I hope you enjoy the cookies. See you around, and have a Merry Christmas." She departed, scooting past the children and running back to the car.

For the rest of the ride, she could do nothing but stare at her own boots, which had become tight for her growing feet but were still warm and without holes.

By the time she and Dorothea arrived back home, Antonina had formed an idea.

"Mama, may I have a new pair of boots? These are a little snug." Antonina bit her bottom lip. If she could get a new pair, these could go to Lucy.

Mama whipped around from the ironing board, where she was pressing one of Papa's shirts. The board and iron shook so hard Antonina held her breath for fear the hot iron would fall and burn the shirt or Mama—or both.

"No." Mama shook her head as she turned back to her ironing. "Your boots will be fine for the rest of this winter."

Antonina's head and shoulders drooped. "Yes, ma'am." So much for her plan.

In front of the mirrors on the chifforobe, Dorothea spun in a rose-colored dress with a fashionable drop-waist and admired herself. Her new shoes and Antonina's were the same style, but Dorothea had received a new dress as well.

Antonina sighed. That dress would be hers someday, Mama had said. Yes, but it would be nice to have a new dress once in a while instead of Dorothea's hand-me-downs all the time. And that rose color would clash with Antonina's red hair. Antonina guessed she was lucky not to have to wear her sister's old shoes too.

Dorothea flipped her dark-brown bobbed hair out of her eyes and tilted her head from side to side. "I think this will do fine for my friends' party and for Mass."

When Dorothea wasn't looking, Antonina crossed her eyes and scrunched her nose and mouth.

Antonina carried the hefty Sears Roebuck catalog to the sofa in the living room and dropped it with a thud onto the velvet cushion.

With a few minutes to relax in private, she could select things she hoped to have in her own home when she grew up. Even the house itself, if she liked one of the house kits for sale. But mostly the beautiful and useful things to go inside it. Including pretty clothes she picked out for herself.

Antonina chuckled as she positioned herself on the sofa. Sal would tease her if he knew how much she liked to dress up now. Or that she thought about getting married and having her own home.

She whispered a quick prayer for Sal and settled the catalog onto her lap. She began to flip through the pages. Appliances, furniture, wallpaper, rugs—saving the women's clothing for last.

Oh. Antonina stopped. Those were like the shoes Mama bought for Dorothea and her, only theirs came from a store in the next town.

Antonina raised her eyebrows. *The price!* The shoes cost as much as two pairs of everyday shoes or boots. She should show more gratitude to Mama and Papa for them. No wonder Mama refused Antonina an additional pair of new footwear.

Antonina continued through the catalog. The pages containing women's dresses, coats, and undergarments were the most fun to look at. With each new catalog in the spring and the fall, Antonina spotted models that resembled women she'd seen, either ladies in Freedom or famous women in the news.

She stopped on one that looked like the actress Gloria Swanson. Antonina laughed. There was the mayor's wife in bloomers!

Antonina continued to smile as she examined individual dresses and imagined herself in each one. At a few of the pictures, she shook her head. Those dresses simply wouldn't do.

She turned a page and leaned forward for a closer look. One of the models resembled Lucy. Antonina blinked. All cleaned up and with her hair fixed but yes, a lot like Lucy. The image mesmerized Antonina. That's what Lucy *could* look like. Would Lucy ever get to dress nice like that?

Antonina clasped her hands, resting them on the pages. *Lord, I know I've asked You for a lot when it comes to Sal and his family, but if You're still listening, I have another request. Please let Lucy's life improve.*

She had to trust that God was listening.

Papa called from the bottom of the stairs. "Antonina!"

Antonina shoved the catalog aside and bounced off the sofa. She ran from the living room and peered over the railing.

"Tell your sister I said to drive you to the Morgan house with this box of food."

"Yes, Papa!" She'd get to see Lucy again. She smiled as she searched upstairs to find Dorothea.

"Can you carry the box by yourself?" Parked in front of Lucy's house, Dorothea blinked rapidly to let Antonina know what the answer should be.

"I'll be fine." Antonina slipped out of the car, opened the back door behind her seat, and removed the box.

Lucy appeared on the porch, smiling, and invited Antonina in before she'd made it up the steps. "It's good to see you again."

Antonina held the box toward Lucy. "There's some bacon in here. And a small turkey."

"Thank you." Lucy placed the box on the table. "My mama said to tell you how much she appreciates everything your family has done for us."

Warmth crept into Antonina's cheeks. *Lucy's family is so grateful for food that Dorothea and I take for granted.* "Tell her we're glad to help." She shrugged.

"And thank you for being my friend." Lucy dipped her chin and spoke softly. "Most of the girls don't want to be seen with me."

Antonina's heart fluttered and then plummeted. How

awful. Because of the way Lucy dressed? Because she had no time to fix her hair or primp like some of the girls? She was so nice, so sweet, so caring of her family.

"I'm happy to be your friend." Antonina squeezed Lucy's arm through a flannel shirt patched in several places.

She needed to act more like a friend to Lucy. The best she could. And she knew just what to do.

Antonina returned home, fearful of Mama and Papa's reaction to her idea.

If the shoes she had not yet worn could be returned in exchange for a sensible pair of shoes for herself, the money left over would buy a pair of boots for Lucy.

At dinnertime after saying the blessing, she broached the subject.

Taking a deep, noisy breath got everyone's attention. She blurted, "Papa, Mama, I want to thank you for the beautiful patent-leather shoes you got me." She exhaled just as noisily.

Dorothea flushed and narrowed her eyes like she was upset she hadn't thought of saying that herself.

"Sweetheart, you are most welcome." Papa sat a little straighter in his chair and beamed at Antonina. He cut into his roast beef and took a bite.

"We're happy we could buy those shoes for you girls. You're both very helpful to Papa and me." Mama's eyes twinkled as she smiled and passed more gravy to Papa.

Antonina cleared her throat. "So I was thinking . . . of

someone who needs shoes worse than I do."

Dorothea rolled her eyes.

"What are you trying to say, Antonina?" Papa set down his fork and glanced at Mama.

Antonina swallowed hard. "Well, . . . if I wanted to return those shoes and get some less expensive ones for myself . . . I could use the leftover money to buy some boots for Lucy Morgan."

Dorothea groaned, and Mama held up a hand.

"She needs them so badly, Papa." Antonina fought tears.

"How long have you been thinking about this?" Papa frowned.

"A while." Antonina's voice sounded like a squeak to her own ears.

"Honey, you know you can't take care of every child who needs a pair of shoes. You're only a child yourself." Mama's eyes crinkled at the corners.

"But can't I take care of one child?" Antonina whispered.

"That's enough." Papa took a deep breath. "Your mama and I will discuss this alone after dinner."

One child. Jesus said when we receive one child in His name, we receive Him.

Antonina and Dorothea cleaned the kitchen and washed and dried the dishes in silence.

From the corner of her eye, Antonina caught Dorothea watching her more than once. If Dorothea were to say

anything, whether good or bad, Antonina would surely start crying. Her heart lodged in her throat, and she repeatedly swallowed hard while she did her chores.

Alone in their bedroom, Antonina knelt at her bedside and gazed at the small crucifix over the headboard. *Please, God, let Mama and Papa see that I must help Lucy.*

Antonina made the Sign of the Cross, bowed her head, and began the Lord's Prayer in a whisper.

When she reached, "Thy Kingdom come; Thy will be done," Antonina raised her head.

His will be done. Not her will. His.

Maybe she was the one meant to help Lucy, but maybe she wasn't. Maybe God had something else planned for Lucy.

Whatever Mama and Papa decided, Antonina would accept their decision as being God's will.

Christmas morning, Antonina stood in front of the chifforobe mirrors. She had never felt so beautiful in her hand-me-down dress and plain, sturdy oxfords.

"Close your eyes," Dorothea said. Her arms circled Antonina's head, and fingers grazed her neck.

Antonina opened her eyes and gasped. "Your favorite necklace!"

"I'm proud you're my sister." Dorothea hugged her. "Enjoy it today, because I want it back tomorrow." She pointed a finger at Antonina and laughed.

"Thank you, Dorothea." Antonina smiled and lifted her coat off the bed.

"Now, let's hurry downstairs. Mama and Papa are waiting in the car, and it's snowing!" Dorothea grabbed Antonina's hand and led her out of their room.

Mama and Papa turned around and smiled when the girls climbed into the back seat. "You both look lovely," Mama said. Papa winked at them.

The family drove to pick up Lucy at her house and take her to church with them. She came out wearing one of Antonina's outgrown dresses, which Mama had taken in to fit her smaller frame, and a new pair of stockings and boots. Like Mama had done with Antonina's oxfords, she'd bought Lucy's boots a half size big so she could grow into them. When both girls outgrew their boots and shoes, they could give them to Lucy's younger sisters.

Lucy's mother was able to come to the door with her robe wrapped around her. She waved and sent Lucy off.

As Lucy settled in the car, her face beamed. "My mama felt good enough to help me wash and curl my hair."

"You look very nice, Lucy," Antonina said. Everyone else agreed.

As Antonina and Lucy knelt next to each other waiting for Mass to begin, Lucy squeezed Antonina's hand.

Lucy's gratitude swelled Antonina's heart. But showing Lucy charity and kindness had required such little effort when all of Antonina's family pitched in their time. In the future, Antonina might have the opportunity to help someone else—a stranger or near-stranger or another friend like Lucy—who needed her. She would seek her parents' guidance again to do what she was able to and then trust God to do the rest.

Antonina blinked back tears and swallowed. If only Sal could receive nothing but kindness from the strangers he now lived among. She'd trusted God to help her help Lucy. He would help Sal, too, and keep him safe. Or He'd use someone who would recognize the calling to help Sal. She was certain.

Antonina needed only one more thing from God this Christmas.

She touched Lucy's arm. "Do you remember Salvatore Scaviano? Sal, from school. Maybe you remember him?" she whispered.

A light shone in Lucy's eyes. "Yes, I do. Your friend, right?"

Antonina nodded. "Would you say a prayer that I hear from him?"

"I will." Lucy bowed her head.

"Mama, what should I do with Lucy's old boots?" Between two fingers, Antonina held up one of the smelly things by its tongue.

Mama paused her dishwashing and eyed the boot. Shaking her head, she said, "I doubt there's any life left in them. Take them to the drum outside for burning."

Antonina stopped to pick up the other boot from the hallway and headed downstairs, then out the back door.

She peered into the pile of debris in the drum. It smelled worse than the boots. She'd add them and start the fire for Papa.

The newspaper Lucy used in her boots would make a good fire starter. Antonina pulled the stuff from one boot, wadded it loosely, and laid it on top of the pile. She pulled out the bunch from the second boot, and a news headline caught her eye.

"Boy rescues smaller child from sewer." She dropped the boot and unfolded the paper, only a shredded portion of a page, but new-looking. Where was this story from? If this rescue had happened in Freedom, or even anywhere in the parish, everyone would've heard about it.

"The boy refused to give his name," she read from the article, "and disappeared into the crowd." Antonina could find nothing on the paper identifying the location. She studied the photograph of the boy pulling his cap down low over his brow, and her breath caught.

Even without seeing his eyes. That face. The set of the mouth. That hand. She'd seen them almost every day for most of her life.

They belonged to Sal.

*_**_**

If you'd like to find out why Sal and his family had to flee from organized crime, leaving behind their friends like Antonina, please consider reading *The Other Side of Freedom*. This historical novel set during Prohibition and widespread prejudice demonstrates the determination and strength of character of Sal, his friends, and family members as dreams are shattered and attitudes

challenged in their rural community. The book has received a number of literary awards, including third place for Children's Books in the Catholic Press Association 2018 CPA Book Awards.

ABOUT THE AUTHOR

In both her contemporary and historical fiction, CYNTHIA T. TONEY writes characters that show tweens and teens how wonderful, powerful, and valuable God made them. Her current project is a novel to accompany *The Other Side of Freedom* that will give readers more of Antonina—and disclose what becomes of her relationship with Sal.

Cynthia is also the author of the Bird Face series, including *8 Notes to a Nobody, 10 Steps to Girlfriend Status, 6 Dates to Disaster, and 3 Things to Forget.*

She is a member of Catholic Writers Guild and Historical Novel Society and is a volunteer with the Independence Italian Cultural Museum in Louisiana. She has a passion for rescuing dogs from neglect and euthanasia and lives with her husband and several canines. Readers can find her on Facebook, Twitter, Goodreads, Pinterest, and Instagram and can also connect with her through her website www.CynthiaTToney.com and her blog www. BirdFaceWendy.wordpress.com.

JUST JESUS

by T. M. Gaouette

"Oh, it won't be Christmas without snow." My friend Kimmy stood at the classroom window and pressed her forehead against the pane, peering glumly out into a dreary but snowless day. Pushing out a deep, heavy exhale, followed by her bottom lip, she twirled back to Trish and me. Then she plopped herself on the desk beside us, dusting the creases from her navy uniform skirt.

The last class of the day, the last day of the week, and less than two weeks until Christmas vacation, and jollity was seriously lacking amongst my high school friends.

"You know, the weather doesn't make it Christmas." Trish pulled a notebook from her backpack and tossed her brown hair back off one shoulder with a flick of her hand.

"Otherwise people in Africa and Australia and all the other hot countries wouldn't have Christmas," I added.

Kimmy combed her fingers down the length of her long, blond hair. "Vanessa, you totally know what I mean."

"I know." I wrapped a consoling arm around her

shoulder. "But we still have Christmas trees and gingerbread houses to decorate . . . aaaand *presents!*" I beamed reassuringly.

I, for one, was totally excited about Christmas. Snow or no snow, I loved this time of year. From Christmas Eve to Epiphany, I was like the queen of Christmas traditions. I could check them off a long list I'd scheduled before Advent had even begun. Ice skating, sugar cookies, volunteering at the shelter, and collecting toys for homeless children. Christmas was a super busy season.

Miss Fitzherbert entered the room and we slid off the desks and scrambled for our seats. Trish bumped the desk next to hers, where a quiet kid named Luke sat. As usual, his head was buried in a book.

Luke lifted his head of dark tousled hair and shifted his eyes to Trish.

She raised a hand and mouthed *Sorry* before slipping into her seat.

"Let's get started," Miss Fitzherbert commanded, scratching the word CHRISTMAS onto the board with yellow chalk.

Facing us, she peered around the room, clad in her usual eclectic ensemble of colors. I'd never imagine pairing a long burgundy corduroy skirt with a burnt orange casual blazer, but at least she had a choice. You could only do so much with blue-and-white-striped shirts under navy woolen sweaters and navy skirts for girls and navy pants for boys. Our individuality lay solely in our hairstyles. Within reason. I wore my dark wavy mess mostly down, tousled with a touch of coconut oil, and sometimes pulled back with a head band.

"What's the *first* thing that comes to mind when you read this?" Miss Fitzherbert asked.

I thought the question somewhat juvenile for high school, but Miss Fitzherbert had a tendency to skim the surface of a profound question to see how deep we could get. Or maybe she just wanted to see if we were awake.

Kimmy shot her hand into the air.

"Kim?" The teacher pointed the chalk at her.

"Love," Kimmy cooed. "But not like just romantic love. I mean like love for our neighbor, you know?"

Miss Fitzherbert bobbed her head and scribbled LOVE on the board.

"Anything else?"

"Family," Danny said from the other side of the room.

An exaggerated sigh gusted from behind everyone. Turning discreetly to see who had the nerve, I caught Trish's stare. She raised her eyebrows, tipping her head slowly toward Luke. The kid was bent over his book, his hair falling over his forehead.

"Great. Anyone else?"

"Charity," Mindy muttered from the front.

A snort this time from behind, still quiet, but enough for me to catch. I twisted toward Luke, who was shaking his head, and when he lifted his face from his page, his eyes immediately connected with mine. Ignoring the fluttering in my stomach—a spontaneous reaction to his steely gray eyes—I wedged my brows low into a scowl.

"Anyone else?"

Facing the front, I whipped my hand up and declared, "Joy." Then turned to Luke with a satisfied smirk.

But he simply leaned back in his chair, dragging his fingers through his hair, and stared at me, clearly amused.

My cheeks burned and I turned to the front.

Kimmy must have seen the exchange, because she leaned toward me, whispering, "Ignore him. He's obviously a Scrooge."

"There's gotta be one, right?" I muttered back.

Besides being quiet and smart and an avid reader, Scrooge was all we really knew of Lucas Hunt, this being his first semester at Saint Augustine's Catholic High School, making us now a class of eleven sophomores. Apparently, he'd been homeschooled. I did find him a tad fascinating, always dressed and pressed well and smelling of cologne—standing in close proximity during a fire drill once had afforded me that pleasurable experience, thank you very much—and his dark hair, a medium-length flow style, with always the perfect amount of wax. Yet he was cold in his demeanor, as if he didn't want to belong. Likely, he thought himself too cool, busying himself instead with reading weird books like *Prince of Darkness* and *Death of a Favorite*. Gross! No, I'd never read them. Who would? They sounded creepy. One thing was certain, he was not a fan of Christmas.

Although a short homeroom discussion, it left a long list on the blackboard that looked similar to my Christmas

to-do list, and I felt somewhat encouraged. Packing my bag, I spared a glance in Luke's direction, wondering what his problem was. Maybe he should consider being kinder. It was Christmas, after all. He caught me staring, and I yanked my gaze away.

The weekend did its usual fly-by as I kept busy with homework, including an essay, in between gift shopping and Christmas-cookie decorating with my younger siblings. Mass on Sunday, then a holiday movie with the family, and it was over! But I was good with it, looking forward to another encounter with the rugged, steely-eyed atheist who was obviously crying out for attention. Maybe my friends and I could teach him a little about Christian charity. He was definitely lacking in that area, with his sighs and scoffs and arrogant smirks. It seemed we had our work cut out for us.

Hushed tones drifted around us when Kimmy and I crossed the threshold into homeroom Monday morning. There was a definite fuss about something, and it didn't take long for us to notice the students discussing the small gifts on every desk, each wrapped in white tissue and tied with a thin gold string. Kimmy and I rushed to our desks to find ours. All the gifts were identical in shape and measured about the size of my hand. I pressed my thumb and finger against the hard, bumpy item inside. The questions continued to float around the room.

"What is it?"

"It's probably from Miss Fitzherbert."

"Can we open them?"

I panned the room just as Luke trudged through the door, his backpack slung over his shoulder. Approaching his desk, he gazed curiously at the gift waiting for him and then at those around him. I quickly averted my eyes but discreetly watched him.

He picked up his gift and handed it to Trish sitting quietly, and seemingly gift-less, next to him. She took it, her cheeks flushing, before setting it on her desk and staring at it.

"Are we supposed to open it?" Kimmy whispered to me.

I shrugged. "I don't know."

Miss Fitzherbert walked in, dropped her bag onto her chair, and glanced at the gift on her own desk.

"Thanks, Miss Fitzherbert," Frances called from the back of the room.

"Well, I don't . . . " She picked up the package, staring at it curiously and then at the students. "These are not from me," she said. "Let's take a look."

Rustling replaced the sound of chitchat as all students tore open their gifts.

I tugged on the end of the tied string, releasing it and unwrapping the tissue paper. I unfolded it to reveal a small baby carved in wood. It was partially covered in a blanket, as if the little guy's kicking legs and moving arms had released him from his swaddled cloth. His short wavy hair, big eyes, and pouting mouth were intricately carved.

He was obviously baby Jesus, and His cuteness caused a lot of *ooohs* and *aaahs* among my confused peers. Comparing our carvings, I noticed tiny imperfections and slight variations in size. Each had been carved by hand.

"Well, these are lovely," Miss Fitzherbert said to the class. "Whom do we thank?" Her gaze searched the aisles, and we all joined her in scanning the room.

No one admitted to gifting us all a baby Jesus, and so we wondered if maybe it was a Secret Santa gift from someone. I stole a look at Trish. Did she know something? Why would she not have received one, unless she was the one giving them out? Maybe she had a wood-carver in the family. What a sweet gesture. I'd catch up with her later.

But catching up with Trish was fruitless. In a quick exchange after class, she revealed that she wasn't the Secret Santa.

I'd been harboring judgmental thoughts about Luke because I'd assumed he'd been rude by tossing the gift back to the giver.

Following a week of classes and after-school Christmas activities, the mystery of the baby Jesus was close to being forgotten. But while Kimmy and I and some others were helping Father John assemble the parish Nativity scene after school one day, I had the shock of my life. The structure was up, Mary and Joseph in place, the manger ready, and even the shepherds and sheep set to go, and I was searching through the last few items in the packing box. I grabbed the next sculpture, unwrapping it as I moved toward the scene. A little leg popped out from under the bundle, and then an arm, and I knew that I had baby Jesus, but when he was fully revealed, my heart did a flip-flop. The design of this baby Jesus was identical to the miniatures that we'd received at school. And this one also was carved in wood, but flawlessly fashioned and painted in now-fading colors. There was no question that whoever carved this baby Jesus had carved the miniature ones too. I rushed to Father, clutching the baby to my heart.

"Ahhh, you found baby Jesus. Now, we'll keep Him in the sacristy until His big day." He took the baby, wrapping Him carefully as he walked.

"Father," I gasped, shadowing him into the sacristy. "Who made this Nativity?"

Father placed baby Jesus gently into a closet. "It's very beautiful, isn't it?"

"Yes, but the artwork is familiar. I have a baby Jesus just like this, and I wonder if the same person made it."

"Well, if I recall, the artist is local." He closed the closet door.

"Really?" I followed him back out of the room.

"Well, he was, I should say. I think he passed a few years back."

"Oh." My mood sank.

"Yes, very sad. But I think his family is still in the area."

"Really?" My mood peaked.

"Yes." Father delved into the packing box and removed another sculpture.

"Does one of them make them?" I pressed.

"Not sure. I can look into it for you though." He handed me an unwrapped angel to set it into the scene.

Following through with his promise to look into it, Father found a name and address, so before heading home, Kimmy and I decided to stop by Secret Santa's house, anxious to discover who was behind the gift-giving.

"He's probably some kind of philanthropist," Kimmy whispered as we ascended the creaky wooden porch steps to the blue door. "Or an ex-teacher who does kind deeds for different classes every Christmas."

"I guess we'll find out soon enough." I raised my eyebrows to ask whether she was ready, then pressed on the bell without waiting for her confirmation. We listened for any movement behind the door. Nothing. I peered around the small front porch, bare but for one white wicker chair and table. A blue sedan was parked out front.

"Should I ring again?" I asked.

Kimmy shrugged.

But before I raised my hand, the door opened and a tall man with graying hair peered down at us over black-rimmed glasses. "Yes?"

"Hello, Mr. Richardson?"

"Mr. Richardson was my father-in-law," the man said, removing his glasses.

I proceeded to introduce us and our mystery as the man scrunched his brow and scratched his stubbly chin. I removed my baby Jesus from my backpack, unwrapped it, and handed it to him. He turned the carving over with the fingers of both hands.

"It's just like the one your father-in-law made for my church's Nativity scene," I said, praying that he had the answer.

The man nodded, a smile softening his features. "Just Jesus," I heard him mutter. But he added nothing else.

"We were wondering if maybe you made them."

He handed Jesus back. "I'm sorry, no. I didn't make them."

"That's strange," Kimmy said. "They're almost identical. We assumed it was a unique design."

"Maybe the artist used some kind of template or pattern," I said, wrapping Jesus carefully.

"I'm pretty sure that he didn't use a template," the man said. "He was extremely talented."

I pressed my lips together. "Well, thanks."

"You're welcome, ladies," the man said with a sympathetic smile. "I hope you find who you're looking for."

The door clicked closed behind them.

It was a bust. Kimmy said it was a sign that we should just put it all behind us.

But I couldn't put it behind me. Maybe I had some sleuthing blood, because I wanted to find the sculptor. Someone had gone to great lengths to send some sort of message, and I wanted to know why. And the question plagued me, even days later in the school cafeteria, as I selected my lunch from the dismal offerings.

"Christmas will be here soon with not a single snowflake in the forecast." Kimmy placed a red apple onto her tray. "It's so depressing."

"Do you think they'd forecast a single snowflake?" I slid my tray along the bar and eyed the fruit cups.

"Funny. Make fun of my sadness."

"I'm sorry, Kimmy." I rubbed her arm. "I just want to see you smile."

"Well, I won't be smiling if we don't have a white Christmas." She grabbed her tray and stormed away.

"Love, family, and charity not enough then?" a familiar voice asked from behind me.

Luke passed close by me, pressing his lips together and raising his eyebrows.

My cheeks warmed and fluttering filled my chest as anger seeped through me.

He meandered around tables and kids to an empty spot by the window.

Fuming, I made my way to Kimmy and the others. But my eyes remained on Luke as he arranged his food, and then—to my surprise—dipped his head to pray.

I thought it a little ironic, from such a cold person, to be honest.

What was his problem? I really wanted to know. So, making a detour, I headed in his direction.

Sucking in a breath, I pushed my shoulders back and strode toward him, feigning confidence.

He didn't see me coming. At least it seemed that way, because his head hung over his lunch and a book, right up until I stood in front of him.

Lifting his head enough to look at me with a questioning slant of his eyes, he said nothing, but waited.

My throat dried up as our gazes connected, and I could only manage to squeak out, "What was that?"

He leaned back in his chair now, setting his book face down on the table and still chewing.

I waited.

"She never mentioned snow the other day," he said finally. "Seems snow is very important when it comes to her Christmas."

"Well, at least she *likes* Christmas."

He just smiled, took a bite of his sandwich, and stared with steely gray eyes into mine. My hands shook, so I rested my tray on the table in front of him to avoid toppling my glass of milk.

"So, I have a question for you," I said quickly, pulling my gaze from his, dragging out a chair, and settling into it.

He waited, eyebrows raised.

"Since you're a closet connoisseur of Christmas, what are your thoughts about the baby Jesus gift mystery?"

He swallowed his bite of sandwich and said, "I haven't really thought about it recently. Why?"

"My friends and I have been wondering about it."

He picked up his book, placing a bookmark into it, and I managed to read the title. *The Dark Tower*. Really? Talk about morbid.

"Can't you just accept the gift and be thankful?" He shoved the book into his backpack at his feet.

"I guess, but why would someone do that?"

"That's what you want to know? Why?"

"You don't?"

He drank from his bottled water and twisted the lid on. "I'd think the message is more important."

"Do you know the message?"

"Yup." He took another bite of his sandwich.

"Mind sharing?"

His eyes sparkled as he chewed, evidently having fun keeping me in suspense. He swallowed and said, "I think it's pretty sad that it's not obvious to you or your friends."

I narrowed my eyes. "I guess you're just smarter than all of us."

Leaning back in his seat, he didn't say anything, as if agreeing with me.

Why was he so rude? He didn't know me or my friends. I was just trying to find out who had given us the gift so I could understand why.

Luke stared at me.

My cheeks burned and I became aware that my hands were in tight fists. But maybe he was right about the message being more relevant. Or maybe who did it really didn't matter at all. Sighing, I pushed my chair back, scraping the floor. I stood and grabbed my tray while looking at him hard.

Without taking his eyes off me, he spoke in a calm, low tone. "My grandfather always used to say that Christmas is about Jesus' birthday, and everything else is either the means to celebrate it or just a distraction."

I held his stare a second more and said, "Fascinating," in a tone that meant the opposite. Then I turned my back on him.

As I stepped away, his voice floated from behind me.

Quieter, maybe more to himself than to me, he said, "Just Jesus."

My mouth dropped open as the familiar words hit my ears.

I spun to face him, splashing milk onto my fruit cup, and dropped my tray on the table. Shoving a finger in his direction, I said, "So, it *was* you."

His own jaw dropped, and he coughed out a laugh. His brow creased as he shook his head.

"Vanessa!" Kimmy called out to me as she approached, Trish close behind. "What's going on?"

"It was him." I continued to point.

But Luke just pursed his lips, pushed his chair back, grabbed his tray, and walked away.

"What was?" Kimmy's gaze followed Luke for a second.

"*He* gave us baby Jesus." I widened my eyes.

"That makes no sense." Kimmy shook her head at me. "How could he be the one?"

"I know." I raised my palms. "That's what I thought—because he got one too."

"He didn't get one," Trish said quickly.

"What?" Kimmy and I spoke at the same time.

Trish bit her lip. "I was the first one in the classroom, and I saw that he didn't have one on his desk. I felt so bad for him that I gave him mine."

"And I *assumed* he didn't want it and gave it to you because you didn't have one." I slapped my forehead with my palm. It made so much sense now. It *was* him.

"He forgot his bag." Kimmy pointed to the backpack still on the floor.

Abandoning my tray, I hurried around the table and retrieved the bag. His book fell to the floor. I picked it up and glanced at the author. C. S. Lewis? Huh! Who knew? My cheeks warmed as I shoved the book back into the bag. Then I rushed after Luke, the girls close behind, trying to catch up with him. But he was on his way back after dropping his scraps into the trash can, probably to recover his backpack.

"Why didn't you tell us that you were the one?"

Stopping in front of me, his jaw tight and eyes narrowed in clear agitation, he said, "Because I *wasn't.*" He extended his hand for his bag, which I handed over.

"Just come clean. We know it's you," Kimmy said.

"Okay, let me say this one more time . . . it was *not* me."

He secured his backpack on his shoulder and headed toward the courtyard exit.

"Of course," I said, chasing after him, deflated and back to square one. "Because you don't even like Christmas. What was I thinking?"

"Who said?" he asked.

"Uh, how about when Miss Fitzherbert asked us what Christmas was all about, and you were all scoffing and shaking your head in the back?" I said, nodding adamantly as if I'd caught him in a contradiction.

"That wasn't because I don't like Christmas," he said, turning to me, his gray eyes ablaze. "It was because of all your responses. And, apparently, I wasn't the only one who thought them dumb."

"Nice!" I threw back at him. "Was Mr. Richardson even your grandfather?"

He pushed through the exit door into the courtyard where the outside chill crushed me.

"You checking up on me?" He threw me a twisted smile. "I didn't know you were interested."

My faced flushed. "I'm not! Just trying to get some answers. Is he?"

"Yes, Mr. Richardson is my grandfather."

"So, if the gifter was not *you*, then who?" Kimmy crossed her arms for warmth.

"Why does it *matter* who they came from?" He shifted his glance to each of us in turn. "It's not about the person who gave it. If it was, he or she would have left a note."

"So, someone decided to carve us each a baby Jesus to remind us all of what Christmas is really about?" I said.

"Like we don't already know." Kimmy added a roll of the eyes to her sarcasm.

"Really?" he asked her. "Which were you? Love or joy?"

"Love." She lifted her chin in defiance.

He nodded. "Love. Christmas is about *love* . . . So, does that mean you'll only love me at Christmas?"

Kimmy opened her mouth as he appeared to wait for

her answer, but her words were evidently stuck in the back of her throat.

A muffled melody of Toby Mac's "Backseat Driver" broke the awkward moment. Luke pulled a phone from his back pocket, eyed the screen while silencing it, and then glanced at each of us. "Sorry, ladies, we'll have to talk about loving me another time."

He started off, leaving us all blushing crimson and looking to each other for an explanation.

Then a question came to me, and with him still in sight, I called out, "Hey, Luke!"

He turned, walking backwards this time. "Yeah?"

"Do you know who did it?"

His grin was wide when he said, "I have a pretty good idea."

As the girls and I stood watching him walk toward the small brick building that enclosed the gym, something light and cold fell on my nose. Barely a flurry, but enough for Kimmy to gasp and squeal, and for Luke to turn in his stride.

His arms out and palms up, he yelled out, "Finally, it's Christmas," before spinning back and continuing on his way.

"That kid is *so* strange," Kimmy said, but her crinkled brow softened as she tipped her head back and closed her eyes, allowing the flakes to land on her face.

I didn't think that Luke was strange. I thought he was extremely frustrating. *Does that mean you'll only love me at*

Christmas? What? What was that all about? And why did he direct that question to Kimmy? Did he like Kimmy? Ugh! Focus, Vanessa! Yes, he was frustrating and arrogant, and how dare he suggest that we didn't know what Christmas was all about. Did he not see the list on the board? Hello! Of course, we did. And if he knew who gave the gifts, why wouldn't he tell us?

Entering homeroom at the end of the day, I marched straight to his desk, where, lo and behold, he was nose-in-a-book.

"If you know who it is, why won't you tell us?"

He sighed and set the book down. "I really think you're missing the whole point of these gifts."

Anger bubbled inside me. I couldn't stand his arrogant face. So, stupidly, I blurted out, "No wonder you don't have any friends."

"I don't?"

"You're always alone."

His eyes still holding mine, he yelled out, "Yo, Jay, we still on for tonight, right?"

To which Jason Turner—one of the more popular boys—responded from behind me, "My place. Bring your A-game."

"Always do," Luke said. All while his eyes held mine, and I sweated profusely under my boring navy sweater.

He smiled.

"You have an answer for everything, don't you?" I said, knowing I sounded as dopey as I felt.

"So, when does the love kick in?" he asked, his face more serious than I'd seen before. "Christmas Eve?"

I tipped my head to the side. "Funny. Here . . . " I placed my baby Jesus on his desk. "It's very beautiful, but can you tell your buddy that I don't need him to remind me of what Christmas is all about, *thank* you very much." Then I turned to stomp away, knocking into the chair behind me a little, but remaining composed. I hoped.

Choosing not to head home right after school, I decided that shopping for last-minute Christmas gifts at the mall would help wash the negative thoughts from my mind and guide me back to the path toward Christmas bliss. But what began as a festive excursion turned sour quite suddenly.

While standing at a jewelry counter, deciding between a necklace and set of earrings for my younger sister, I inadvertently heard a random mom's conversation with her daughter. The two moved hastily along the counter toward me. Their eyes scanning the offerings beneath the glass as they spoke.

"So, *when* then?" The young girl—maybe a couple years younger than me—leaned on the counter and dropped her head low.

"Honey, I don't know." The woman pressed her hands on the glass, her voice tightening, her attention on the selection. "We're supposed to be at Uncle John's by five for dinner Christmas Eve, so there's just no time. And if we don't open the gifts first thing on Christmas day, we won't have things cleaned up and lunch ready by the time Grandma and Grandpa get to our house. What else could we possibly fit in?"

The girl straightened to face her mom, crossing her arms. "So, then this will be, like, the first Christmas I *don't* see my cousins."

"Well, it was Aunty Jenny who decided to move further away." Her mother's eyes never left the items in the display case. "I invited her, but she wants Christmas at her place, and I want Christmas at ours . . . so, I don't know what to tell you."

"Well, what about the day after Christmas?"

"Honey." The mother finally looked at her daughter. "Can we *please* not do this right now? I'm just trying to find something for Cathy at work." She resumed her search.

An exaggerated sigh escaped the young girl's lips. "What are you even looking for?"

"Honestly, at this point, I don't care. So . . . let's just pick something and get out of here."

Every sentence crushed me. Each so sad, empty of the true meaning of Christmas.

And when the mom finally looked up, her expression weary, we accidentally connected eyes. It was hardly a second, but it was enough for me to capture her story, and it broke my heart. Yet, it wasn't dissimilar to mine.

In this woman's stress; in my long Christmas to-do list; in Kimmy's desire for snow, we all missed the big picture.

They were right—both the Secret Santa and Luke were right. And I couldn't sleep all that night, thinking about how right they were. I hardly ever thought about Jesus during Christmas, except when reminded: at Mass, or when assembling a Nativity scene . . . or when receiving a carved baby Jesus as a gift. And how often did that come about? I was doing the things I was supposed to do and acting in a manner I was supposed to act, but just at Christmas and certainly not yearlong when I was too busy making assumptions and judging boys by the books they read. Always missing the obvious! *So, when does the love kick in?* I'd shown no love in my unrighteous judgment of Luke, thinking him unchristian, rude, and friendless. All of which I'd been so wrong about. Love, hope, joy, family . . . those were things we should live and celebrate every day, not just at Christmastime. No, I wasn't mad because I was insulted. I was mad because he was right, and I was embarrassed. I had lost Jesus along the way, and I needed Him back. *Take me back, Lord.*

Next morning, back in homeroom, I walked more humbly to his desk, feeling the gaze of my friends watching from afar. He glanced up from his book and smiled. Not a mean, arrogant smile, as I'd have characterized it maybe yesterday and every day before, but a kind smile that I knew I didn't deserve. At least not after everything I said to him yesterday. I sat in Trish's chair, and he waited for me to speak.

"I'm sorry," was all I could muster in a low pathetic

murmur.

"I forgive you." His eyes sparkled.

"I'd . . . I'd like my baby Jesus back, if that's all right with you."

Smiling, he retrieved the carving, still wrapped in white tissue, and handed it to me.

I opened my gift, brushing my thumb over baby Jesus' blanket and head before wrapping Him back up and putting Him into my backpack.

As I stood, Missy, a homeroom classmate sidled over to us and settled onto Luke's desk. Seriously? Could she get more familiar?

"Hey, Vanessa," she said. "Watch out for this guy. He's trouble."

I didn't hang with Missy or know her very well, but she was pretty. That and her confidence just rubbed me the wrong way.

"I guess you should know," I said, my words harder than I'd intended. Ugh! What was wrong with me? I was a definite work in progress!

Luke must have recognized the tone too, because he lifted his chin, his eyes narrowed, his jaw tight. Had I hit a nerve?

"Oh, I do," Missy said, giggling, and evidently missing my snipe. "I'm his cousin after all, so you let me know if he gives you trouble. I'll put him in his place."

Boom! A multitude of thoughts exploded in my mind. His cousin! *Relief.* My assumption! *Another* stinking assumption! *Shame.* My rudeness! *Embarrassment.* Letting

God down. *Guilt!* Thoughts and feelings all at one time, bounced off each other, and then . . . *truth!* His *cousin?* Did that mean she . . . ?

I snapped my gaze to Luke, whose steely grays were already on mine, as if he knew every thought in my head, every feeling in my heart, and that big looming question. And I knew what he was asking in the silence of his stare. Does it really matter? Does it?

No! Suddenly it didn't matter who or why. What mattered was the message. What mattered was who I'd become and what I'd forgotten, and both were sad revelations. Love and joy and charity were wonderful things that *originated* from the ultimate Christmas Gift from the ultimate Giver, but they were for *all year round,* not just for Christmas.

Not that *Jesus* was just for Christmas—but if I wasn't baking Christmas cookies for His glory, then what was the point? Because Christmas wasn't Christmas, could not be Christmas, without Him!

Christmas is about Jesus' birthday and everything else is either the means to celebrate it or just a distraction.

And boy had I been so extremely distracted, every single day of the year and right through Christmas, to the point of forgetting that the only thing that really mattered was Jesus. Just . . . Jesus!

*_**_**

Sometimes the answer is not as obvious as we'd like. Sometimes we have to search a little deeper for it. This may be true for some readers of "Just Jesus." This element of discovery is characteristic of T. M. Gaouette's fiction and inspires a desire to think a little more deeply when it comes to knowing, loving, and serving God. Gaouette also enjoys bringing two characters together from opposite ends of a faith scope, making for a fun story with surprising twists. For more stories with exciting twists and colorful characters, reflecting God's mercy, check out her *Faith & Kung Fu Series*.

ABOUT THE AUTHOR

T.M GAOUETTE is the author of the *Faith & Kung Fu* series for young adults, as well as *The Destiny of Sunshine Ranch* and *For Eden's Sake*. She also contributed to the last Catholic Teen Books anthology, *Secrets: Visible & Invisible* with her short story "Sister Francesca." Her novels have received the Catholic Writers Guild Seal of Approval (except new releases for which the Seal may be in process). Born in Africa, raised in London, England, Gaouette now lives on a small farm in New England with her husband, where she homeschools her four children, raises goats, and writes fiction for teens and young adults. A former contributor for *Project Inspired*, Gaouette's desire is to instill the love of God into the hearts of her readers. You can find out more at www.TMGaouette.com.

A VERY JURASSIC CHRISTMAS EVE

by Corinna Turner

JOSHUA

Skating gently across the frozen lake, keeping my speed in check, I ready myself—and execute a little spin. Without falling on my rear. Yes!

I'm improving, but progress is slow, because I get only a few days to skate each year. Dad and Uncle Z drove north for a Christmas break every year since I was seven, just so that I could skate out in the open countryside instead of inside one of the looming, crowded urban rinks further south. Those invariably sent city-phobic me—wilderness-raised boy that I am—into a panic.

What was it like in the old days, before the crazy scientists and their arrogant assumption that they could contain the creatures they'd bred? Hard to imagine, and I don't waste time trying. So what if the world outside the fenced cities is harsher and more dangerous than it once was? It's my home, and I like it as it is.

Ecstatic at my achievement, I spin again—successfully!—and tear off down the center of the lake, gathering speed. I love the feeling of flying over the ice, so fast, so free. Out here on my skates, I could outrun even a raptor.

Of course, the rest of the pack would box me in fast enough, which is why the biggest Christmas gift Dad and Uncle Z gave me, year after year, wasn't the fuel, but their time, as they sat up there in the Habitat Vehicle's turret, getting anything but a holiday themselves as they kept watch over me. Uncle Z's up there now, carrying on the tradition. Only one pair of eyes, the last two years, but that's how it is now.

Pushing away the sadness that twists in my stomach at the thought of Dad, I bend my knees and pile on the speed even more, my heart pounding with healthy effort. I'm sixteen now, and after nine years I can stay up on my feet really well, but I'm only just getting to grips with the fancy maneuvers. I'm certainly not gonna try to spin going at this speed!

The icy wind whips in my face, fluttering my coal-black hair against my forehead, though I always cut it before it's long enough to get in my eyes and block my gun sight. Yes! This is the life. Okay, so I prefer the milder climate of Exception State, really. But I do so love to skate.

"No closer to the far shore, Josh." Uncle Z's voice startles me, coming from my earpiece.

I raise my head, my concentration broken, wobbling slightly as my eyes scan the snow-blanketed bushes,

slopes, and beach coming up ahead.

"Whoa!" I jam my right skate in front of my left one, bringing myself to a rapid halt, heart pounding even harder.

Emerging from the nearest undergrowth is a . . . yes, a fully grown female allosaur, thirty feet long with a mouth full of razor-sharp four-inch teeth. Uncle Z laughs his head off in my ear, entertained by my emergency stop. He let me get nice and close on purpose, didn't he?

"Very funny, Uncle Z! Aren't you supposed to be on watch?"

"I'm keeping watch better than you, dreamer boy," comes the chortling reply. "Well, she's a skinny, mangy old creature, ripe for culling, doncha think? Let's not look a Christmas gift in the mouth. Bounty on an allo will pay for some of that fuel we burned coming all the way up here."

I eye the huge predator. Same upright conformation as a raptor or T. rex, though far bigger than the largest raptor species and only a fraction of the size of a T. rex. Resembling a rex more than a feathery raptor with her bare, leathery hide, only a crest of display feathers tops her head. She's thin all right, her ribs showing starkly, but I'm close enough to see that she's *not* old. Or mangy. Just starving. Why? She's moving well enough, and there's no wound that I can see.

She stops at the edge of the frozen lake, stretching her head toward me, nostrils flaring. Close to drooling. Oh yeah, she's hungry.

She actually raises one big clawed foot and places it tentatively on the lake, then draws it back as a creaking boom sounds from the ice. I'm perfectly safe. She's far too heavy to venture out here. She stretches her neck, shuffling her feet, never taking her eyes from me. Having a meal so close is torture.

"Ah, I'll put her out of her misery for you," says Uncle Z. "Stand still until I give you the all clear."

I hear the *chink* of Uncle Z's rifle touching the bars around the turret as he makes sure the muzzle is unimpeded, then the snap of his safety catch coming off. My earpiece will filter out the volume of the shot, so I need only stand and wait.

Something moves in the bushes behind the hungry allosaur. What the . . . ? Surely it can't be . . . ?

But it is!

My hand flies up, palm flat. "Stop, Uncle Z!"

"What's wrong?"

"Look. Coming out of the bushes . . . "

They're fully visible as they toddle down the beach, one, two, three of them, clustering around the female's stocky legs.

Allosaur chicks. The female is a hungry mom.

DARRYL

"How are things going, Darryl, my girl?" calls Dad as I approach the family room.

"Things are as ready in the kitchen as I can make them," I tell him as I enter, wiping my hands dry on my jeans before reaching up to re-tie my shoulder-length brown hair. "Soon as people begin arriving, we can start warming the cider. Half an hour before, we can slide the pecan pies into the oven. I put the cream in the jugs already and the plates are stacked, everything's ready."

"Good job. Can you help Harry with the chairs while I go drive the fence early?"

Yeah, I was expecting he'd do it now. He won't want to later, and it's better to check it before we have a load of extra people on the farm for the evening. "Sure, Dad." But my heart sinks a little. I was kinda hoping that with the catering all ready I could go drive the fence with him, have a few minutes off. I love when it's our turn hosting the Christmas Eve carol service, no mistake, but I've been on my feet working from dawn until . . . well, it's not dusk yet, but the sun's certainly dropping in the sky. "Is Father Ben here yet?"

"No, not yet."

"I thought he said he'd be here mid-afternoon?"

Dad shrugs. "He sent a heads-up when he left as usual—taking the mountain road—but he's running late. He should've come over the last pass half an hour or so ago, so he'll be here any time."

Distress signals rarely make it to the satellite from that winding minor road through the towering mountains that split Exception State in half, and the timid or less experienced driver will invariably drive all the way around on one of the main highways. But it's a really significant shortcut so Father Benedict, being neither timid nor inexperienced and with four wheel drive, invariably heads straight up and over.

Since it's actually only a carol service, not Mass, Father Benedict's kinda optional, but he'll preach a good homily, and he sings nice and loud. Some folks, like Dad's childhood friend, our neighbor Maurice Carr—who claims he only comes for the refreshments—aren't that enthusiastic at belting out the carols.

My insides clench at the thought of the Carr family. Maurice's wife, Sarah Carr, is really sick and won't be coming tonight. But she's insisting that Uncle Mau bring the children, just as usual. It's no secret, though, that all four Carr children will be as motherless as Harry and I, within a few months. Which is worse, knowing it's coming or having your mother snatched from you in an instant in some stupid farm accident? I shake my head. There's no good way to lose your mom, especially when very young.

"Right, I'm fence-bound." Dad traipses out, passing my younger brother, Harry, staggering under an armful of the folding chairs we use for Sunday Mass.

I head to the hall cupboard to fetch more. It's the only event of the year when we need every last one.

"I wonder why Father Ben's so late." Harry pushes his shorter brown hair behind his winter-pale ears with both hands as I return with my own armful of chairs.

"Something came up, I guess. Well, he'll be here any minute. Let's finish this and get our afternoon chores done."

Soon enough we've squeezed all the seats we can into

the family room, spilling out into the doorways to the hall and dining room, and we're putting the finishing touches to the decorations.

"There." I straighten a big red bow on the front door and put my hands on my hips with a satisfied nod. The farmhouse's steel shutters are all open, proclaiming the efficiency of our twin Renfield Ozone 4 electric fence, and Dad's even circled the turret on top of the house with little fairy lights. Harry, having arranged a cheerful Christmas hat on the head of the little statue of Saint Desmond on one side of the door, is carefully draping the dainty, red velvet cloak that Mom made years ago around the Our Lady statue opposite. "I think we're ready. Let's get the chores done, then we can shower and change and hang out with Father Ben when he arrives."

"Okey-dokey." Harry bounces off toward the barn as though he hasn't been working just as long as me.

"Don't forget to check on that sick edmontosaur in the handling barn," I call after him.

Was I that energetic at eleven? I mean, fourteen's hardly old and decrepit, is it? I sigh, reflexively check my ScreamerBand, although I'm outside already—no alarms have been tripped, the fence remains unbreached and secure—then head to the young stock barn.

Soon, I'm dropping the calf feeder over the side of the bovine pen. I give only a few quick scratches to the eager butting heads as they crowd forward to drink, then trundle the much bigger 'milk' trolley along to the other, larger half of the barn, where the 'saur calves are kept carefully separate from their fragile mammalian bottle mates.

Plugging the pump tube into the milk trolley—which actually contains green liquid feed mix, but it's the same consistency as milk so we tend to call it that—I switch it on, then lean over the fence, looking into the pen—lowered, of course, like all 'saur handling pens, though here the concrete walls drop only two meters. "Dinner, y'all," I call. A pair of two-month-old male edmo calves—brothers—and a single female iggy calf, all three already as tall as I am and weighing five times as much, lumber up to the feeder. The twins latch onto a teat each, while Janey the iggy raises her flat head level with me, her beaky mouth parted hopefully.

"Just a quick scratch," I tell her, obliging. "I've got to hurry!"

I rub the itchy spot behind her jaw for a few moments. "Okay, enough, Janey. Go have your milk."

I've no bovine calves left to individually feed, but one runty little iguanodon is still on the bottle. I move to the end pen and let myself in, clucking encouragingly until the gangly little male iggy gets to his feet and totters forward as I step inside the safety ring. Only coming up to my chest and being very weak, it's still safe to come in here with him. A bigger calf could crush this little metal rail just by leaning on it too hard.

"Good boy." I offer him the bottle, and he takes the teat readily. He can graduate to the feeder soon. I don't scratch him as he feeds, except for massaging his chin to encourage him to start sucking again when he loses interest. It's not a good idea to make pets of male stock. The few top quality males we kept as stud animals are always sold to other farms, with only good, sound females remaining here as breeding stock. Janey is in with a good chance of staying, if she carries on growing so well.

Soon, he's emptied his bottle and, after checking him over, I'm collecting the empty milk trolley and calf feeder and heading back to the mix room to wash everything. I'll feed my charges again just before bed—probably with a gaggle of hyper younger guests trailing after me, tonight—and again first thing in the morning, Christmas Day or not.

Reaching the farmhouse again, I eye the empty yard and frown, my stomach chilling. Still no Father Benedict. Where is he? I check the time on my ScreamerBand. Only an hour until the service is supposed to begin and well over an hour since Dad said he'd arrive any minute. Heading inside, I'm checking the House Control console for messages when I hear Dad's farm truck stop in front of the house. He's done with the fence.

"Anything?"

I glance over my shoulder, shaking my head, as Dad strides into the house. "Nothing. Just his heads-up message from earlier."

Dad's mouth tightens, and he raises his ScreamerBand to his mouth, pressing the talk button. "Harry, get back here and grab your rifle. We're going to find Father Ben."

He lowers his wrist and glances at me. "Darryl, start the . . ." He hesitates, and I can guess what he's thinking. The hunting truck has a rudimentary turret, allowing better defense, but the normal road truck has stronger towing capabilities. Father Benedict's van is a heftier vehicle than some mere car, and there's little doubt now that he's stopped somewhere in the mountains. *Broken down* being the far preferable scenario than *crashed*, though both are extremely dangerous.

Dad makes a face. "Start the road truck, I guess."

Yeah, neither vehicle is perfect for this.

"And do the safety checks," he adds.

Okay, he's really worried if he's going to trust me to check the grilles and wheel shields so we can get away quicker. Dad always does the checks himself.

As I place a hand on the scanner of the gun locker, he presses the 'record' button on the console and starts leaving an audio message saying where we've gone and asking our neighbors Riley or Maurice, whoever arrives first, to finish preparing the refreshments and entertain everyone until we return. It's almost a two-hour drive to the far side of the mountains plus forty minutes to reach the first pass, though I'd bet Dad's about to do it in thirty. We're going to be late getting back.

My hand trembles slightly as I lift my rifle from the rack and head outside, Father Benedict's bright eyes and cheerful laugh filling my mind.

Lord, please let us be in time.

JOSHUA

"What the—" Uncle Z bites off a word Saint Des

wouldn't approve of. "You messed up crazy 'saur, what you wanna go and hatch out chicks for in midwinter? How'd you even do it? Build your nest near the hot springs, huh? No wonder you're skin and bone, missy."

The allosaur ducks her head to check the chicks at her feet, then lifts her gaze to me again. She's clearly in dire need of food herself, but it's her chicks she wants me for. It's kinda touching. Not that I'm offering or anything.

"She's a good mom, though. Hasn't abandoned them yet."

Uncle Z snorts. "Or gobbled them up."

Yeah, many carni'saurs aren't great parents, especially if things get remotely tough. Allosaurs aren't the worst, but they sure ain't the best, either. "Well, I'm really impressed. Do we *have* to shoot her?"

"So am I, Josh, so am I, but she won't survive much longer without either cutting those chicks loose or eating them herself."

"Well, she hasn't eaten them yet."

"Okay, so say she doesn't eat them? All four of them will be dead in another week or two. Look at the snow. Prey's scarce; they don't stand a chance. Best thing we can do is cull the mother and catch the chicks. A zoo will be happy to have them."

Chink. He's raised his rifle again. But it seems such a cruel reward for her efforts. "Aw, come on, Uncle Z, it's Christmas! Can't we just catch them and leave her?"

A long silence in my ear. I'm asking him to pass over a good-sized bounty. The Dinosaur Activity and Population department (or DAPdep, as most people call them) don't like hungry allosaurs prowling.

Mama Allosaur sniffs the breeze and begins to pace around the lakeshore, the three miniature versions of herself stumbling along behind. Little carni'saurs like that, they should be bouncing around. They won't last much longer.

"Oh, fine. We'll try it, anyway. Now git back in here before she cuts you off."

Yeah, she's definitely moving to check out the HabVi. It's impossible to completely avoid odors remaining around a vehicle you live in all the time, all you can do is keep it down enough that it's too slight to interest something as large as a rex. An allosaur won't manage to break in, though she could do some damage trying.

Getting cut off is something I take very seriously these days, so I spin and skate quickly across the lake. Mama Allosaur shifts to a lumbering run, trying to keep up, so I pile on the speed until she falls behind. If she's too close when I come to shore, Uncle Z will have no choice but to shoot her.

She's only halfway around the lake's curve when I reach the bank, over which looms our armored house on wheels, with its huge off-road tires and full observation turret on top. Of course, struggling up a steep bank of frozen mud in ice skates is slow, but removing them would be even slower. But she's still at a comfortable distance when I let the side door hiss closed behind me and hit the lock button.

Unlacing the skates quickly, I pull them off. Huh, the brown skin of my fingers is almost blue with cold. That'll teach me not to wear gloves!

I scramble up the ladder to the turret without bothering to put my boots on. "How are we gonna catch them?" I ask, peering down. The mother is just approaching the 'Vi, the chicks straggling well behind.

"Unseal a pack of meat and chuck it in the rear pen. Then open the lower door section only."

Yeah, let the chicks come in, but not her. "Okay, I'm on it."

I slide back down the ladder in my socked feet—already chilling in this frozen climate—and grab a scent-sealed pack from the meat locker. It's the work of a moment to cut it open, place the contents in the back of the rear pen and lock the inner pen door again.

"Are the chicks here, now?" I call.

"Yep. 'Round her feet again. Open sesame."

I double-check the inner pen door, twice more—the way Dad and Uncle Z drilled into me from the moment I could reach the lock—and only then press the outer door control, lower flap only, looking through the observation hatch as it opens. A small square of daylight appears on the floor of the pen.

Right. Come on, chicks. In you come. You must want that meat. The chicks should rush right in, too young to be wary—

Mama Allosaur's big head appears in the opening, nostrils flaring.

No, don't you—

She sticks her muzzle in, grabs the meat and whips her head out again.

Argh! So much for being such a good mother! She'll have eaten that meat in one gulp! Fuming, I scramble back up to the turret. "Did you see that? What a . . . " I look down, and three little heads dip and raise and swallow as they tear pieces from the meal their mom's just provided. Oh. She took it for *them.*

"Uncle Z . . . " How can we split them up? It's *Christmas.*

At my tone, he shoots me a suspicious look. "What?"

"Couldn't we . . . I don't know, take them *all* to the zoo?"

His head jerks back. "*All?* The mother too? Since when were you so spatially challenged, Josh? We cannot fit an adult allosaur in our rear pen, and that's a fact. And the 'Vi would only just carry her weight."

"Nooooo . . . but . . . it *would* carry it. And . . . "

His glare deepens. "What?"

"Well, we could fit her body in the living area and her head in the rear pen. I mean, with her sedated and tied down, of course."

His lean, muscled hands drop onto his hips, thrusting out his belly, which is showing the effect of the lifelong diet of prime fried steaks that neither Dad nor I have ever managed to persuade him to give up. "And her *tail?*" he demands.

"Well, uh . . . that would have to go in, um . . . "

"My bedroom?"

"Yeah." The cab 'bedroom' has always been Uncle Z's. "Only place for it." I mean, no way to drape the tail up into my over-cab bedroom.

"You know what that means?"

"Um . . . that you hate the idea?"

"Well, yeah, I do, but it also means I'd have to sleep in with you the whole way to whichever zoo was having them. And the best zoos—most zoos, period—are all further south, so that'll be several days, especially so heavily laden."

That dents my enthusiasm for the idea. Sometimes I can hear Uncle Z snoring even through my soundproofed floor.

"And the other thing . . . " Uncle Z smiles a little too broadly, like when he's about to clinch a deal. "We can't keep that monster tranqued for more than two, three days tops, without causing her serious harm—or running out of drugs. So, say we do bring her on board with the chicks, then we have no choice but to pull up stakes at once and drive south, non-stop, spelling each other at the wheel, right through Christmas Day and the day after, to get her delivered alive and healthy."

He looks me straight in the eye. "So if we take her, the holiday ends right now. No more skating. No relaxing over Christmas. Just a 'Vi overflowing with carni'saurs, three of them trying to eat our fingers every time we take our eyes off them and the other near certain death if we get the dosage wrong."

He smiles even more. "So Josh—it's entirely up to you."

DARRYL

I check the time on my ScreamerBand as we swing off the main highway, climbing toward the first pass. Twenty-seven minutes. Dad's worried, all right.

"Start keeping your eyes peeled, kids," he says, as the land falls away to our left, an increasingly dizzying drop opening out to the valley floor.

"We always keep our eyes peeled!" In the rearview mirror I catch the indignant frown Harry throws Dad. "Oh, come on. You know what I mean."

I swallow and start paying close attention to that precipitous slope below. Yeah, Dad doesn't want to say straight out, *start looking down there for a smashed-up van.* No one could survive coming off the road here, not without a miracle. I make sure to spare the odd glance up the slope and around. Most of the 'saurs up in the mountains are fairly small—well, small to medium—but you do get the odd allosaur or similar-sized herbi'saur. Hitting something that big would bring our rescue mission to an abrupt—maybe permanent—end.

We clear the first pass, and there's the road ahead, visible—mostly—all the way to the second pass. No sign of Father Benedict. Where is he?

Dad drives as fast as he dares, every ounce of his attention on the winding road as he steers into the corners, accelerating down every straight bit. *Yeah, come on, Dad. Faster, faster!* We've got to get right over that second pass, now, before we can hope to find him. How long has he been stopped for already?

Something moves high on the upper slope, like a cloud of small specks rippling across the rocks. Just a shoal of itsy-bitsy piranha'saurs. Deadly in those numbers, though.

I swallow. Raptors aren't the only threat to a smashed-up vehicle. In fact, piranha'saurs can squeeze inside far more quickly.

Dad must sense my churning anxiety, because he says, "Let's not blow this out of proportion, kids. Father Ben's got his priest hole, remember?"

True. The diocesan-issue sleeping vans aren't designed for overnighting unSPARKed—outside of an electric fence—they just give an itinerant country priest a berth any place without a spare bedroom. But like all the best vehicles that clock up many hours of unSPARKed travel, they have a small, man-sized compartment down in the chassis where the driver can take refuge in the event of a breakdown. Raptors have been known to break into the refuges, but only when help has been slow arriving.

So long as Father Benedict's been able to crawl in there, then even if he actually crashed and the vehicle was compromised from the moment he first stopped, he's got a few hours' extra time. Still . . .

Come on, Dad. Can't you go any faster? Not that I want to end up at the bottom of this mountain, either.

Finally, we're climbing to the top of the second pass. Still three more to go. But any moment now, we'll get to see at least some of the road ahead.

There's nothing, though. *Agh! Lord, please look after him. He works so hard for You.*

We're probably God's answer, though, aren't we?

Father Ben, we're coming as fast as we can!

We round several more corners, the last one so fast that Dad slows down a little for the next. Drat.

But the steep bends give way to a gentler curve, the road disappearing out of sight around a shoulder of mountain. More of the road comes into view as we get further along.

Wait! Is that . . . ?

"Dad, something's glinting. Where the road's visible over that outcrop."

"Let's hope it's a windshield."

Yeah. An *intact* windshield.

JOSHUA

My gaze travels to the great frozen lake we're parked beside, the memory of flying over the ice filling me. We only got here yesterday evening. After Uncle Z slept in and we ate a leisurely lunch, I've barely been on the ice for an hour. If we leave now, I won't get to skate again for a whole year. I'm old enough to know that any resolution to grit my teeth and go to a city rink will come to nothing. I love skating, but not more than I hate cities.

I turn to the little family below us. The mother's nose hovers just over the chicks and the fast-disappearing meat, nostrils flaring with longing, but she still doesn't snatch it from them. She would win allosaur mother-of-the-year award, no question. How can we take her chicks away and leave her? Okay, she'd probably get over them quick enough, but now she's in such bad condition her survival's far from guaranteed, in this climate.

"No more skating would stink, eh, Josh? It's a long time 'til next Christmas." Uncle Z's worried by my silence.

Oh, I want more skating. I do . . .

But there's a mother down there who wants her *babies*. My mother didn't want me. Did she, heck. But that little family down there we can keep together, if we're only prepared to put up with a few uncomfortable days.

But what about the skating?

I glance at the little image of Saint Des hanging over the front of the turret windows. Saint Des, the patron saint of hunters and anyone who lives out-city. Saint Des, so holy he lived with the raptors for twenty years, unharmed. *Don't be selfish, Josh*, his calm gaze says. *Especially not now, at Christmas.* Okay, so they're just vicious carni'saurs. But they're still God's creatures. Saint Des even splinted a raptor's leg once, didn't he?

"Let's take them," I say.

Uncle Z's jaw drops. "Josh . . . "

"You just said it was up to me. I say we take them."

As a frown settles on his face, inspiration strikes, and I add hastily, "Just think what they'll fetch. A perfect little family, completely out-of-season. No zoo will have naturally hatched 'saur chicks for three months, yet. Talk about scarcity value. And with a dramatic rescue story to go with them. What a winter attraction for the zoo that gets them! We'll hold an auction, right?"

From Uncle Z's sudden intent look, I've finally hit upon a reason for him to put up with this. He always was less sentimental than Dad. In fact, if *he'd* been my dad, I doubt I'd be here, not that I've ever doubted his love for me growing up. But it's just him and me, now, and we've still gotta balance the books, preferably without hiring an assistant to share our little moving home. Yeah, we're happier with just the two of us. Even if that means it has to be the six of us, for a few days.

He draws a deep breath, and I hold mine.

"Alright, Josh. You win. I'll get the tranquilizer gun. But this is gonna be one heck of a miserable Christmas." He swings down onto the ladder and shoots me one more glare. "And if I wake up Christmas morning with one of those things eating my nose, I'm blaming you."

DARRYL

As we round the outcrop, the source of the glint comes clearly into sight. It's Father Benedict's van. Pulled barely off the single-track road into a passing place, a little higher up the mountain. It doesn't look scrunched or bent, from here, just parked, but . . . my insides clench. Long, feathered tails wave from open doors. Dakotaraptors. I count four, just from here. Probably more inside and round the back.

"Ugh, should've brought the hunting truck," mutters Dad. "Well, break the windshield, Darryl, quickly."

On this narrow road, it's impossible to shoot through

our side windows, and what's a little glass compared to Father Benedict's life? I grab the hammer and whack it into the center of the windshield. Cracks appear at once, so I raise my feet and kick until the whole thing crumbles into little pieces and rains down over the dashboard and into the foot wells, bouncing off Dad's white knuckles as he clutches the wheel.

Harry's already leaned between the seats and poked the muzzle of his rifle through the windshield grille by the time I've righted myself and lifted my own gun.

Crack.

The range is long, and Harry's first shot kicks up a puff of dust to the right of a tail. I throw a quick glance up the slope at some straggly, windswept trees. Yeah, they're moving. "There's a stiff westerly breeze, Harry. Compensate."

Taking my own advice, I aim slightly to the left of another tail and fire. The tail jerks violently, and a large male raptor with blue-green ruff feathers backs out of the van and leaps around, feathers flying from its tail as it bites at the injured spot. I ignore it and line up my sights on the next tail. Right now, I just want as many of them away from Father Benedict as possible and distracted is as good as dead.

Crack. Harry's shot goes wide again, but only just. I say nothing, this time. He's trying his best and piling on pressure won't help.

Crack. My next target recoils from the vehicle. Ah-ha, a big female, yellowy-brown ruff. The pack matriarch? I try to get her in my sights—take her out and they may all run—but she's too quick. The instant her questing eyes fix on our approaching vehicle she darts behind the black van, calling sharply to the others. Heads pop from every door—*ah, thank you!*—I manage to hit one. So does Harry.

With an urgent screech, the matriarch breaks cover and streaks up the mountainside toward some crags. Just as I fire she takes one of her species' infamous, lightning-fast twenty-foot leaps, landing unharmed behind the sheltering rocks.

The surviving six raptors race after her, three adults and three juveniles—last spring's chicks, no doubt. I manage to drop the one I injured first, which is moving slowest, and Harry grazes another—DAPdep will have to get some hunters in to do some culling. Then they've all vanished among the crags, though I sense beady eyes watching us. If we put a foot wrong, they'll drop on us like lethal rain.

Dad stares up at the crags, frowning. He puts his hand on the window controls and drops all the side windows so Harry and I can shoot at the pack if they return.

I join Dad in eyeing the road ahead. There might just be enough space left in front of Father Benedict's truck for us to turn around. I glance at the drop and try not to gulp.

Inching alongside Father Benedict's van—there's barely room for a car to pass—Dad spins the wheel and backs up to the mountainside until we feel the thick rubber bumper nudge the rock. Spinning the wheel again, he pulls forward, peering through his window as the side wheels

. . . well, it certainly feels like they're skimming the cliff edge. I try to loosen my grip on my rifle. It's not going to help if we go over, is it?

And then . . . phew, we're back in the middle of the road, and Dad's quickly backing up to Father Benedict's van. There's a click as he unlocks the trunk door. Then he looks from me to Harry, his lips tightening. Yeah, as the oldest, most experienced, best shot, able to provide the best cover, he needs to stay here. That means Harry or I needs to hook up the tow cable. And I'm a far better shot than Harry. *No . . .*

Harry licks his lips nervously, though his eyes brighten with heroic delight. "I'll do it."

"No, I can do it." I grab Dad's arm, but Harry immediately grips his shoulder.

"I can do it, Dad! It'll only take a second. And Ryl's a far better shot than I am. She has to provide cover."

Dad looks at me and makes a face. Yeah, though it kills him to let eleven-year-old Harry go out there, it's gotta be that way. This is no time for sentimentality. Harry will be safer with me and Dad covering him than I'd be with Dad and Harry for cover.

"Okay, Harry. But wait until I tell you. Just hop down, snap the winch hook into the tow ring and leap straight back into the truck, you understand? It doesn't matter what you see or think you see if you get a closer look at the van. You jump straight back in. Got it?"

Harry nods.

"You'd better. Because one of those raptors could be

down here in about three seconds, and you know how hard it is to hit one in midair."

Harry nods again, more earnestly. Yeah, if a raptor comes down here, it will probably end up dead, but it might kill Harry first. Even without a bullet in her tail, the matriarch will be too wily to risk it, but a wet-behind-the-ears juvenile might disobey her. Let's hope she's a bossy-boots.

Dad and I take up our places by the side windows—me in the back and Dad in the front so we can drive straight off—and get our rifles into the best positions. We're kind of having to ignore behind us, but nothing large could possibly come up that precipice.

"Okay," says Dad. "Harry, go."

The rear door opens toward the cliff, unfortunately, providing no protection for Harry. Jumping out and crouching in the gap between the vehicles, he grabs the winch hook, turns and snaps it into Father Benedict's front tow ring. Giving it a yank to check it's secure, he straightens . . .

A shadow flits across the van. A second later, my eyes find the lethal-clawed shape springing down the slope, wing-arms spread for extra lift. One more leap, and it'll land on Harry!

Dad's rifle cracks, but the juvenile doesn't stop.

I aim, not even taking the time to breathe.

Lord-don't-let-me-miss!

JOSHUA

"I'd say she's about five thousand pounds." Uncle Z measures off the correct dose of sedative from the bottle. "But under the circumstances . . . " He draws out a quarter as much again.

It's quite an overdose, but I make no objection. I've been so busy worrying about the 'saur family, only now do I think about *my* family. An *adult* allosaur *inside* the 'Vi? This isn't exactly the safest stunt to be pulling.

I try not to bite my lip as Uncle Z waits for Mama-allo to be downslope of the chicks—in the hope she won't topple on them—then lines up the sights on her skinny thigh and pulls the trigger.

She starts, nudging the dart from her skin at once, but the force of the impact will have emptied the drug straight into her system. For a few minutes she stands, shaking her head, then she staggers. After only ten minutes, she goes down, but we monitor her for another ten minutes. No movement.

"Right." Uncle Z speaks decisively. "If we wait any longer a pack of raptors will probably turn up and eat all four of them. I'll go and see about winching her in. You close this hatch and don't open it until I tell you, understood?"

I do bite my lip, this time. Somehow, I pictured us both securing her, looking out for each other on the ground, but of course, with just the two of us, one of us has to provide proper cover. My sentimental whim is putting Uncle Z at risk, and if it's Mama-allo or Uncle Z, I'll choose Uncle Z any time.

"Maybe this isn't such a good idea, after all. Maybe we should just grab the chicks and—"

Uncle Z snorts. "Oh no, you don't. Those four are a whopping Christmas gift from Saint Des, and I should've realized that myself. Just try and keep half an eye on her as well, will you?"

He slides down the ladder, shutting the hatch firmly behind him. In a few minutes he lets himself out the rear door, clutching our Utahraptor-sized metal-mesh muzzle—the largest we own—and some chains.

Okay, so we're not looking your gift'saur in the mouth, Saint Des, but . . . please don't let it bite Uncle Z's head off? Sleek, glossy, bright-eyed please?

DARRYL

Alerted by Dad's shot, Harry turns and dives for the trunk just as I fire.

The juvenile twitches midair, but crashes down on Harry, its weight dragging him back outside, where it lies on top of him, thrashing. I start to swing my gun round, but the shot could go through and hit Harry.

Snapping the safety catch on with my finger even as I reverse the rifle, I leap onto the raptor, slamming the butt into its head as hard as I can, trying to stun it. No, all I've got to do is . . .

I wedge a foot against its neck and shove its head to the ground, clear of Harry. It jerks, wild, uncoordinated, almost throwing me off. I've just got to hold it down long enough for—

Crack!

Dad's bullet takes it cleanly through the head and it's finally still.

"Harry! Are you okay? In, *quickly!*"

If he's so much as grazed himself on the pavement, the other juveniles won't be able to help themselves at the smell of blood.

"Fine . . . Jus' stuck . . . " Panting, he struggles to get out from under the dead raptor.

I try to lift it, feathers coming out in my hands, but it's too heavy. Dad absolutely cannot come to help or we'll have no cover *at all*. Ah-ha! I drag some of the tow cable from the winch, heave the raptor's head up so I can wrap it around its neck, then press the external winch button.

Whirr . . .

The winch isn't high off the ground, but it lifts the carcass enough that Harry finally manages to scoot out from under. I shove him up into the vehicle, then dive in behind, swinging the door closed.

Click.

Safe. *Thank God!*

JOSHUA

I keep half an eye on Uncle Z as he cautiously approaches the—apparently—unconscious carni'saur, gives her a few pokes, then moves close enough to whip the muzzle over her nose. It fits over the very end of her mouth—*just*—though he can't use the snap-catch and has lengthened the straps already. That in place, he secures her legs with normal chains, since the padded restraints we use on larger raptor species—which will only fit in the pen when sedated and folded in—are too small. We can take the chains off for a few minutes later and see about oiling her hide and wrapping some bandaging around to prevent sores. Right now, we just need to get her safely inside before any scavengers show up.

In between scanning the surrounding landscape for threats, I take a few peeps on the internal cameras at Uncle Z.

He opens up the rear pen completely, stowing the dividing wall, then hooks the winch cable to her ankles and draws her in. Plenty of cursing as he gets the huge tail stowed in his cab room, and I grin. Then he winches her in slightly further and finally gets the rear door closed.

Huh, so much for worrying about how to catch the little nippers. They've followed Mom straight into the 'Vi. I'm itching to go below. In fact . . .

"Josh? Get down here and deal with these little fluffballs! I can't lash this beast down with them chewing on my elbows!"

Great! I open the hatch and slide down, grabbing the nearest chick in time to stop its sharp little baby teeth closing on Uncle Z's posterior. Again, by the look of his pants.

"Oh no, you don't!" The gaunt baby is about knee-high and squirmy. "Where shall I put them? Critter cages?"

"Nah, they need to stay right close to their mom or they

won't smell right and she'll reject them. We'll have to leave them loose. Just keep them off me." He yanks another strap tight, securing Mama to heavy rings in the 'Vi floor.

"Okay. Come on, you three, stick with me." They're kind of cute. In an —*ouch*— sharp, pointy way. I get them some more meat and start teaching them to take it nicely and not bite me, an achievable goal since we've got them so young, although right now it just involves a lot of nips from them and plenty of slaps to their noses from me. "What shall we call you, eh? Two little boys and a girl. Hmm."

I eye their mother. "Well, *you* should be called Star, 'cause you're a star mom." The crest feathers on her head are even a yellowy orange. "Yeah, and it's Christmas. So that means you three should be, hmm . . . "

The chicks are downy all over, though one day they'll have bare hide same as their mother. I touch the female's head, the fluffy beginnings of longer orangey crest feathers soft under my hand. "So, I name you Gold." I move my hand to the two males in turn, greenish fluff and cream fluff. "Frankincense and Myrrh. What do you think, Uncle Z?"

He grunts, hauling on another strap. "Couldn't care less."

"Well, you should. Good festive names will just make the zoos even more eager to get them. And you did call them a gift from Saint Des, so we should appreciate them."

"All right, they're good names, a great present from Saint Des, I'm setting up the auction as soon as I'm done with this; I'm properly appreciative, really. Just teach them not to bite before you worry about teaching them their names, or our chances of having any sort of Christmas dinner are *zero*."

"I'm working on—*Ouch!*"

Uncle Z chuckles. "Oh, and Josh?"

I suck my bleeding finger. "Yeah?"

"Merry Christmas."

I stop trying to remember how many boxes of scentBlock bandages we have in the medicine kit, a smile stretching my lips. Yeah, it's dusk now, it's Christmas! And things aren't going badly, are they? We've got all four of our hapless guests safely aboard without anyone—in either family—getting eaten. Star is snoring hard and almost completely secured, and we've even named them! Okay, so it's gonna be one weird Christmas, no mistake, but . . .

It's still Christmas, right? And wasn't the first Christmas all about trekking off somewhere they didn't really wanna go, with a baby on board? And they ended up sleeping in some sort of tiny mammal-stock barn, didn't they, cheek to jowl with the animals? With the baby in the feeding trough, which I picture looking something like the little soundproofed box Dad used to pop baby-me in if I started crying at a dangerous moment. Yeah, you could say we're doing Christmas properly this year. Authentic travel and scramble and stuff we'd rather wasn't happening.

Which are we, though? The family . . . or the

innkeepers? Huh.

Well, it's a *proper* Christmas, either way—even if we'd rather it wasn't.

"Merry Christmas, Uncle Z!"

DARRYL

The truck's engine roars as we tow Father Benedict's van—and the dead raptor—along behind us. We've winched the vehicle right up to our bumper, lifting the front wheels off the ground to side-step the handbrake, which is surely on.

"You really are okay, Harry?" Dad asks over his shoulder. "The claws didn't get you?" Although clearly desperate to get in the back and hug us both, he started driving at once. Father Benedict could be hurt or *anything*, back there. Time to get emotional later.

"Fine, Dad." Harry's still panting slightly. "Phew, when that thing dropped from the sky and landed on me . . . " He shook his head. "I thought I'd had it. But it just wriggled around like it wasn't even interested in me at all!"

"It probably wasn't," says Dad. "Seeing that your big sis had just put a bullet in its chest." He shoots a glance up at the slope, now smooth, open, and treeless. "Right, this is a good spot." He draws to a halt and puts the handbrake on, then eyes Harry and me with the same look as earlier, his gaze fixing on me.

Yeah, we're not likely to get surprised here. Plus he doesn't want Harry to see . . . what might be seen, inside the van. "I'm on it, Dad."

"I can go." Harry sounds less enthusiastic than earlier, but willing.

"Darryl's turn. Get your rifle and find a good position to cover her."

"Okay." Harry obeys so meekly he's clearly still shook up. Who wouldn't be? When a raptor lands on you, you don't normally walk away.

Soon as they're ready, I ease open the side door, far side from the slope, and slip out, darting quickly along to the nearest free-swinging van door. I slip inside, not stopping to pull it shut. It's as likely to impede my exit as keep anything out, in its current condition. The dusk lighting outside provides little illumination and I peer through the gloom as my eyes adjust. The place is trashed, fridge door hanging open, but no sign of Father Benedict. Or blood, thank God.

Where's the priest hole? I don't dare call to him. A loud shout will carry too far and a quiet one will make me sound even more like prey. My fingers trace over the floor. There! A fiddly little lever, and another, and one more at the bottom. I get them up and slide the hatch away.

Father Benedict! He's there. Slightly younger than Dad, he lies on his back, one arm clutching two books to his chest, the other crossed neatly over it with his rosary looped around his dark brown hand, as though he's waiting to be buried. His springy, tightly curling hair is as neat and unruffled as ever and almost as black as his clothes, his clerical collar making a little spot of white in the dimness. His eyes are closed, his face peaceful. *O God, don't let him be hurt!*

I grab his shoulder. "Father Ben?"

He gasps; his eyes fly open, fix on me. A huge relieved breath comes out of him. *"Darryl!"*

"Come on!"

He's already sitting up, scrambling out. He's right behind me as I lead him straight back to the truck. And then we're inside, the door closed.

Slumping in a rear seat, he shuts his eyes for a moment, his lips moving silently. Still clutching his books and his rosary.

"What'd you bring those for?" asks Harry.

"He had them in the priest hole with him," I say, annoyed with him for risking his life by taking the time to save them.

Father Benedict opens his eyes at last and smiles. "They're *leather-bound.*" He displays them, his Bible and prayer book. "Raptors would chew them to shreds. And this . . . " He pools the rosary into his palm. "Well, I *needed* this. My SOS signal, you know. My lifeline. Worked, didn't it?"

Harry grins, and I can't help smiling too.

"Were you *asleep,* Father Ben?" I have to ask.

He reddens. "Ah, no. Not asleep. Just, er, composing myself." At our blank looks, he mumbles, "I thought the raptors were getting that hatch up at last, is all."

That doesn't mean much to Dad and Harry, but remembering the peaceful look on his face . . . it strikes me deep.

I don't have time to dwell on it, because Dad climbs into the back and drags Harry and me into his arms at last. We both put out an arm and scoop Father Benedict into the hug too.

"I don't need a *single other gift* this Christmas." Dad's voice shakes slightly.

"Nor do I." My voice muffles against a shoulder.

"Me neither," says Harry, with feeling.

"Nor I!" says Father Benedict—most fervently of all. But after only a moment, he adds, "Hmm, much as I hate to break this up, aren't we supposed to be welcoming the Divine Infant with joyous song right now?"

"We are," says Dad. "Let's get underway, then."

I poke Father Benedict and give him a firm look. "*You* are having hot cider and a slice of pie before we begin!"

"We all are." Dad speaks even more firmly.

"I won't say no to that." Father Benedict's hand shakes slightly as he gives mine a quick squeeze. "*Christus natus est. Deo gratias.*"

"*Deo gratias,*" I echo.

"*Deo gratias,*" murmur Dad and Harry.

Christus natus est. Christ is born.

Let nothing distract us from *that*, huh, Father Ben? Not even a pack of hungry dakotaraptors. Priorities and all that.

Christ is born.

And life goes on.

Deo gratias.

*_**_**

To learn whether Darryl and her family manage to have an uneventful Christmas and to find out what befalls Joshua, his Uncle Z, and their dangerous passengers Star, Gold, Frankincense, and Myrrh on their long journey south, look out for the full *un*SPARK*ed* Christmas special, A VERY JURASSIC CHRISTMAS, coming Summer 2020. Or grab DRIVE!, the first *un*SPARK*ed* story, now. To meet Joshua again, make sure you read on to the second story, A TRULY RAPTOR-OUS WELCOME! And don't miss the unSPARKed prequel, BREACH!, about Josh's dad, his Uncle Z—and baby-Josh!

ABOUT THE AUTHOR

CORINNA TURNER is the author of the *I Am Margaret* and *unSPARKed* series for young adults, as well as stand-alone works such as *Elfling* and *Mandy Lamb and the Full Moon* (for teens) and *Someday* (for older teens and adults). All of her novels have received the Catholic Writers Guild Seal of Approval (except new releases for which the Seal may be in process). *Liberation* ('I Am Margaret' Book 3) was nominated for the Carnegie Medal Award 2016 and *Elfling* won first prize for 'Teen and Young Adult Fiction' in the Catholic Press Association 2019 Book Awards. Several of her other books have been placed in the CPA Awards and the Catholic Arts and Letters Awards.

Corinna Turner is a Lay Dominican with an MA in English from Oxford University, and lives in the UK. She has been writing since she was fourteen and likes strong protagonists with plenty of integrity. She used to have a Giant African Land Snail called Peter with a 6½" long shell—which is legal in the UK!—but now makes do with a cactus and a campervan. You can find out more at www.IAmMargaret.com.

BOOKS FOR TEENS & YOUNG ADULTS
BY THESE AUTHORS

CAROLYN ASTFALK
Rightfully Ours

T.M. GAOUETTE
The Destiny Of Sunshine Ranch
Freeing Tanner Rose
Saving Faith
Guarding Aaron
For Eden's Sake

KATY HUTH JONES
Treachery and Truth

THERESA LINDEN
Roland West, Loner
Life-Changing Love
Battle For His Soul
Standing Strong
Roland West, Outcast
Chasing Liberty
Testing Liberty
Fight For Liberty
Anyone but Him

SUSAN PEEK
A Soldier Surrenders:
The Conversion of St. Camillus de Lellis
Crusader King:
A Novel of Baldwin IV and the Crusades
Saint Magnus, the Last Viking
The King's Prey:
Saint Dymphna of Ireland

CYNTHIA T. TONEY
8 Notes To A Nobody
10 Steps To Girlfriend Status
6 Dates To Disaster
3 Things to Forget
The Other Side Of Freedom

CORINNA TURNER
I Am Margaret
The Three Most Wanted
Liberation
Bane's Eyes
Margo's Diary
Brothers
The Siege of Reginald Hill
Someday
Drive! *(Unsparked 1.0)*
A Truly Raptor-ous Welcome
(Unsparked 2)
BREACH! *(Unsparked Prequel)*
Elfling
Mandy Lamb and the Full Moon

LESLEA WAHL
The Perfect Blindside
eXtreme Blindside
An Unexpected Role
Unlikely Witnesses
Where You Lead

For more authors and titles, visit CatholicTeenBooks.com.
And subscribe to our newsletter for new titles *hot off the press!*

www.ingramcontent.com/pod-product-compliance
Lightning Source LLC
Chambersburg PA
CBHW051919110726
47902CB00002B/335